LP BRIDE  11/oy

Bride, Johnny Mack.
Horse thieves : Johnny   ck
Mack Bride.

$\mathcal{A}$ 6

34

HORSE THIEVES

Jim Parry was a skinny, peaceable man who was going out to California to find work as a store clerk. However, after being stranded in Buckshot, Nevada, he got the idea of starting a mule-train haulage business instead. But then somebody stole his two saddle horses and he faced disaster. But Parry had a stubborn streak in him and a number of hard men were to find out that he wasn't known as Mule-Head Parry for nothing.

JOHNNY MACK BRIDE

HORSE THIEVES

Complete and Unabridged

LINFORD
Leicester

First Linford Edition
published 1998
by arrangement with
Robert Hale LImited
London

The right of Johnny Mack Bride to be
identified as the author of this work has been
asserted by him in accordance with the
Copyright, Designs and Patents Act, 1988

British Library CIP Data

Bride, Johnny Mack
    Horse thieves.—Large print ed.—
Linford western library
    1. Western stories
    2. Large type books
    I. Title
    823.9'14 [F]

ISBN 0–7089–5323–9

Published by
F. A. Thorpe (Publishing) Ltd.
Anstey, Leicestershire
Set by Words & Graphics Ltd.
Anstey, Leicestershire
Printed and bound in Great Britain by
T. J. International Ltd., Padstow, Cornwall

This book is printed on acid-free paper

1

Harness creaking, iron shoes clinking, the mules hiked their way up the stony mountain trail, six of them, young animals and fit as mountain goats. Behind the string stalked a saddle horse, a chunky bay gelding bare of any rig but a halter and behind that followed a short, thick buckskin carrying a rider.

The rider held a coiled lash that he shook out from time to time and cracked inexpertly over the heads of his mule team. The mules ignored the threat because they knew, as mules do, that they were doing all right and, anyway, the Montana sun had begun to sink in the sky and that, if things went as they normally did, they'd be stopping soon and their packs would be unloaded and there would be water and a roll in the grass and grain, because they'd been pulling hard.

Two pairs of eyes watched the cavalcade as it pecked its way up the steep trail and, thirty feet higher up, another two pairs of eyes watched the watchers.

Joe Bad Water turned his head towards his partner and grinned. "Two good horses an' six mules. An' there'll be other stuff, plenty of it. We'll do all right." He nodded, partly to reassure his partner, partly to reassure himself. A quarter-breed, Joe sat in a broken saddle on a skinny, pinto pony, his nail-bitten hands holding the worn ropes that served as reins leading to the string-mended bridle. His clothes were store-bought but worn and tattered and meant, long ago, for another man. "I'll maybe even get me a pair of boots." His feet, hanging down low for the want of stirrups, were dirty, bare and calloused.

Moon Dog grunted. "Guns? He got guns?"

A different character, Moon Dog.

Pure Comanche and bad tidings all the way through. An outcast from his tribe with the sinister glance of the natural delinquent, he forked a fifteen hands bay gelding, stolen from the US Cavalry. His legs were encased in deerskin leggings and his bronzed torso was covered by a piece of horse-blanket with two holes cut out for armholes. An ancient flintlock musket, held in his two lean brown hands, rested across the withers of his mount.

"Maybe . . . maybe," Joe Bad Water stalled. If there was a gun he'd want it for himself. But he couldn't see Moon Dog going along with that. And it didn't pay to cross Moon Dog. Besides, he needed the Comanche. Moon Dog had balls. You could get stuff if you were with Moon Dog. If Moon Dog hadn't taken him along . . . well, truth was there'd be nowhere to go. White folks wouldn't have him — and Indians wouldn't have either of them.

But with Moon Dog at least you could get stuff. Horse now and then — saddle, harness, tools — stuff you could sell. An' with money, well, you could get anything with money. Whisky — oh yeah! They weren't unwilling to sell him whisky, as long as he had the money and went to the right place. An' there were women, too, who would take the money. Joe thought with hungry yearning of the whores in Buckshot. Yeah, life was better with Moon Dog. But you had to watch him. He could cut up rough and you never knew the minute . . . "Yeah, there might be a gun," he nodded. "An' if there is you can have it. You can give me that one." He nodded towards the ancient flintlock. Shit! It was a piece of junk but what else could he do?

★ ★ ★

Thirty feet higher up the mountain, hidden by a screen of thin bushes, the two white men looked down at the action below.

"They're after him aw'right," said

Brandy Lee. "Could move in on him any time." A thick-set, hard man of forty-five with worn, store-bought clothes and scuffed cowboy boots, he squatted on the parched earth, his two hands, broken-knuckled and meat-coloured, taking the forward weight of his body as he peered down in the sun glare. "They know they got an easy mark."

"Yeah." His partner spoke thoughtfully. A lean, dirty-blond man of around thirty in worn, trail-soiled town clothes. His face was burned red by the sun except where an old knife scar stood out livid white from one ear to the corner of the mouth. The long, tow-coloured hair almost concealed the fact that the upper half of one ear was missing. Jack Holt stood up slowly, easing his stiff limbs. He reached for the reins of the horses ground-haltered behind them then paused, thinking aloud.

"It might not be a bad idea at that . . . "

Brandy Lee glanced up at him, his face a question mark.

"I mean, if we let them raid that mule train? If them two Apaches stole all his stuff," Holt went on, "we could move in after . . . take the horses. They'd get the blame. We'd be in the clear. Boss wouldn' mind. He'd be happy."

Lee heaved himself to his feet. "They ain't Apaches," he said. "One's a 'breed. You've seen him aroun'. Other one's a Comanche."

"You know what I mean," growled Holt.

"Yeah, yeah, don't get sore," said Lee. "I see what ya mean." His expression changed suddenly. "But they might find a gun or two among those packs. They'd be armed. Maybe dangerous."

"Who? Joe Bad Water? Dangerous?" Holt snorted contemptuously.

"Maybe the other guy. The Indian. We don't know. Some of them can be kinda sharp."

6

"He tries to get sharp with me, he's dead," grunted Holt. "But maybe you're right. We won't take no chances." He put a foot into a stirrup and heaved himself into the saddle. "Let's do it." He neck-reined his horse around then checked and looked back at his partner. "An' remember, we don't take nothin' but the horses. Right?"

Brandy Lee leaned forward in the saddle. "But he's sure to have other stuff. Good stuff. We're takin' the horses, we might as well take the mules. Mules fetches good money." He studied his partner's face for a moment then said guardedly, "Boss don't need to know about the mules. Jus' you an' me."

Holt looked at him. "You really think Sammy wouldn't know? You don't know Sammy — an' you wouldn' want to know him if you tried somethin' like that. Naw. We do as he says: we wait till night, take the horses an' leave ever'thin' else. We don't take nothin' else, understan'? No guns, no

7

saddles, no money — nothin'. Jus' good ridin' stock. Got it? Them's the boss's orders."

Lee shrugged. "Sam's the boss," he said resignedly.

"An' don't you forget it!" grunted Holt.

★ ★ ★

Old Joe Carney spied the mule train from the top of the hill above his mine. He left his work gladly and set out to meet it halfway: it wasn't every day that he got supplies and enjoyed company.

"Well hello an' right welcome!" he called, when the train was still fifty yards away. He waved a shovel in one huge hand, the iron on it worn down almost to nothing. "I been lookin' out for you for days." He continued talking as he walked to meet them, talking with the pleasure of a man who spends much of his time alone.

The rider on the buckskin kneed his mount out of the line and rode forward to meet him. "You Mister Carney? Joe Carney? You ordered shovels? An' cotton thread an' needles? Rheumatism pills an' other stuff?"

"That's who I am, son, an' them things is all for me, Joe Carney. An' you got somethin' else too, I figure. Coupla bottles of White Lightnin'?" Old Joe took hold of the buckskin's bridle and fell in alongside as, followed by the mule train, they made their way to his camp.

"Oh, yeah." The rider seemed to pause awkwardly. "'Bout the whisky. I think it was on that mule that went over the cliff."

Joe stopped in his tracks. "Aw, don't tell me . . ."

The rider's face split into a grin. "No. Your whiskey's all right, Mister Carney. I'm a-joshin' you, that's all."

Joe looked up in pleasure at the joke. He saw a young man, a rather unusual young man for these parts. His clothes were newish and good and he sat in a good saddle on a good horse, but somehow he didn't seem to fit the part. His face, for a start, was beardless and soft-looking; his hands too looked soft, not the hands of a regular mule-skinner, nor those of a cowboy or a miner. His teeth were good too — too good for someone who had lived long in Montana — and his voice and way of speaking were — well, different. Altogether there was something about him that suggested he was from much further east, from somewhere civilized, where life was easier and people had the time and means to take care of their bodies.

"Well, 'long as you got that whiskey you can break it out, an' we'll try a little of it, you an' me. See that it hain't gone bad or nothin'." They were approaching Joe's camp.

Joe let go of the buckskin's bridle and stepped aside to slap the rumps of the mules as they passed, pointing them in the right direction. "You'll stay a while?" he asked. "I got coffee brewin' an' it won't take me no time to rustle up some stew an' beans."

The rider was dismounting stiffly. He held out his hand. "Jim Parry." They shook hands and the young man gestured to the mules standing with heads hanging in the late afternoon heat. "Parry's Cross-Country Haulage."

"That's it?" The old man smiled tolerantly.

"That's it today." The young man too was smiling. "But one day I'll have a hundred mules and fifty wagons. I'll be haulin' freight all over America."

"Well, if that's what you want, son." The old man went into a rickety shack and came out carrying a stew pan which he filled with water. "You hungry?"

"Sure am, Mister Carney. Be a pleasure to eat with you. But I don't know about stayin' long." He looked at the sky. "I got plenty deliveries to make, long ways to go yet."

"Take it easy, son. Sun's goin' down already. Ain't wise to travel in the dark in these parts. You'd do better to rest yourself an' your animals. Make better time tomorrow."

"Well, I'll be glad to eat with you, anyway." Jim Parry unsaddled his buckskin, rubbed the animal's back with a gunny sack and tethered him to a scrawny tree. "You see to the grub an' I'll see to these critters."

★ ★ ★

Joe Bad Water and Moon Dog drew rein in the shelter of some high rocks. "We wait till dark?" Joe looked questioningly at the Comanche.

"Uh." The Comanche nodded. "Wait here." He slipped from his mount's back, ground-haltered the animal and squatted down with his back to the sun-warmed rock.

"But we ain't got no water here." Joe stayed mounted, his belly empty, his mouth parched. "We could ride over there," he jerked his head over his shoulder, "an' make camp. Could eat. An' drink. We got plenty time."

12

"Wait here," grunted Moon Dog without moving.

"Sh — " began Joe, then he grumbled, "I don't see that we got to . . . " He began to slip from his pony's back and stopped suddenly as his bare feet hit the ground. He stood stock-still, listening, then gestured silently to Moon Dog with a jerk of the head. There were sounds some way off.

Moon Dog rose silently and took up the old flintlock. He felt for the hunting knife in its deer-hide sheath at his belt, a knife that had already ended three men's lives. Joe Bad Water felt for his own knife. Together they waited in silence: maybe the sound didn't concern them.

The sound came straight towards them and the people making it weren't bothered about keeping quiet. Moon Dog raised two fingers to indicate two riders and Joe Bad Water nodded. The sounds came closer, then very close then two white men rode around their

13

protective rock and let their horses stop, just a couple of yards from them. They sat looking at them without speaking.

Joe Bad Water had a bad feeling. One of the men was Brandy Lee, a man to be feared. He didn't know the other one's name but he had seen him around Buckshot. He rode with the same crowd. Joe tried a weak smile but there was no response from the two men. The silence continued and Joe knew that the longer it lasted the worse things were.

"What you dogshits doin'?" Brandy Lee spoke with casual contempt.

"Nothin'." Joe tried not to be afraid. He was glad Moon Dog was with him.

"You ain't got no ideas about that mule train, them horses?" Jack Holt kneed his horse forward as he spoke and shoved it right up against Joe, pushing him back a couple of steps. There was a spasm of sudden movement. Moon Dog stepped quickly and lightly aside and brought up his old flintlock.

In immediate response, Brandy Lee spurred his mount violently, charged forward, shoving Holt and Joe Bad Water aside and riding Moon Dog down. In an instant he was out of the saddle. Moon Dog was struggling to rise. Lee leapt on his back like a cougar, caught him by the hair and hauled his head back until it seemed his neck would break. He held a long knife, blade worn thin with much honing, at Moon Dog's throat. "You wanna play rough, Injun? You figurin' on shootin' me?" He shoved the blade against the Comanche's throat and a thin line of blood showed. The Indian was still, petrified like rock.

"Naw! Naw!" Joe Bad Water could not stop himself. He ran towards the two men, hands held up, palms forward. "Don't! Don't do it! We ain't thinkin' 'bout them. Ain't lookin' for no horses nor nothin'. We're huntin' a bear. Been huntin' him two days." He stopped, wondering if he would be alive in two minutes' time.

Brandy Lee looked at him thoughtfully, not relaxing his hold on the Indian, the knife still held at his throat. After a few seconds he nodded slightly. "That right?" The voice was mockingly casual. "Well . . . " He looked towards Jack Holt who was still in the saddle. "Seems these fellas are huntin' bear, Jack." He paused then said, "What do you think?"

Holt appeared off-hand. "Could be." He looked around with casual indifference at the rocky terrain. "Bear country aw'right."

"Well, maybe so." Lee spoke into the Indian's ear, the knife still held at his throat. "Maybe they weren't lookin' at them horses at all. Maybe that mule train got nothin' to do with them bein' here." He looked towards Joe Bad Water again. "They'd goddamn better be. 'Cause if I thought they was meanin' to try to steal them horses . . . " He raised the knife slightly until it was just under the Indian's nose and made a deft cut between the nose and upper lip. Blood ran freely down the Comanche's chin. "I'd cut their goddamn balls off, both of 'em." He let go, shoved the Indian forward violently and stepped back. "Now get the hell outa here! Both of ya."

He walked heavily towards his horse, the knife still in his hand. Moon Dog scrabbled on the ground for a couple of confused seconds like a 'coon tipped out of a sack then, snarling like a cougar, sprang after him, leapt through eight feet of space and landed on Lee's back. Both of them went tumbling down in a hot, heavy, struggling mass.

Jack Holt swung out of his saddle and lumbered forward, drawing his pistol from its holster. Joe Bad Water sprang for his pony, leapt aboard and went clattering wildly away — anywhere, just to be out of there.

Lee and the Comanche were struggling furiously in a cloud of rock dust, first one on top then the other. Holt tried to grab hold of the Indian but could hardly distinguish one limb from another. Then in a split second's pause he grabbed the Indian by the hair and brought his pistol down on the dark head. There was a sound like a hammer hitting soft rock and the Comanche's body went limp.

Brandy Lee shoved out from underneath the slack body and struggled to his feet spitting and cursing. Holt was holding his pistol barrel right against the Indian's head, the hammer thumbed back.

"Naw!" spat Lee. He jerked his head over his shoulder. "The sound could carry to that camp." He cast glances over the dusty earth, looking for the knife he had held. It was lying three feet away, half covered in dust. Lee lumbered forward, grabbed the knife and almost without straightening up swung towards the unconscious Indian. He grabbed the long hair, hauled the head backwards and drew the thin blade deeply across the brown throat from ear to ear.

Holt watched with mild curiosity.

18

"What about the other one?" He jerked his head in the direction of the fleeing Joe Bad Water.

Brandy Lee considered. "Naa." He wiped the bloody knife on the dying Indian's clothes. "He ain't no trouble. He's too goddamn scared to do nothin'. Anyways, he don't count. Nobody goin' to take no notice of anythin' he says. And like I say, he's too goddamn scared."

"Let's get out here," growled Holt. "I ain't makin' camp alongside a dead Indian. An' I sure as hell ain't buryin' him."

They remounted. "There's water back there a ways," said Lee. "We can eat. An' sleep a little. We gonna be workin' durin' the night." He grinned. "We got horses to steal."

★ ★ ★

Old Joe Carney had been around. He'd fought in the war and had once been talking to, and looking into the eyes, of a Reb soldier at exactly the moment that the soldier was shot dead. Sometimes, on bad nights when he couldn't sleep, he remembered the terrible look on that soldier's face, the unbelievable shock, the dreadful knowledge in the eyes that life was over, that death had claimed him. Joe thought of that incident again when he beheld Jim Parry next morning. The man looked as if he had died inside, while walking around.

"What in all hell is wrong?" Joe cried. Parry's face was death-white, his head hung low and his shoulders sagged deeply. He might have been shot dead but still standing.

"My horses." His voice was a dying croak. "They're gone. Stolen."

Joe's first reaction was one of relief. "You ain't hurt? Ain't got no arrow in you? Ain't been snake-bitten? You sure?" He walked quickly round the young man, looking for visible damage.

A slow, heavy shake of the head. No other comment. The youngster looked as if he might fall down. God knows what's holdin' him up, Joe thought.

Joe took another breath. He needed it, after a shock like that. "Horses gone?" he said. Well, Jesus! That was bad! But it wasn't as bad as . . . Joe hitched up his pants.

"You're sure they're gone? he asked. "Ain't just wandered off somewhere?"

Jim Parry shook his head. He was only half the size that he'd been yesterday, with his shoulders slumped and his head hanging like a lead weight. "They're gone. Gone. I been lookin'. All over." He sat down on a rock and Joe thought he might still just fall over and die.

"Come on. We'll look again." Joe hauled the young man to his feet and they set off on a new search.

But the two horses were gone. Stolen. Joe knew it, because hobbled horses didn't wander off leaving no tracks: the leather hobbles tying both forefeet together cause a horse to move in heavy plunges, leaving deep tracks in the earth. Someone must have cut the hobbles and driven the animals off. Strange, too, the mules were still there, and all the other stuff. So it was professional horse thieves, men who took only prime stock. Real professionals.

"Well, coulda been worse," said Joe. They were seated at his camp-fire. He'd made coffee and laced it heavily with White Lightning in an attempt to put some spirit into this broken young man. "You still got your mules, an' all your other stuff."

"But no horses." The man was beyond consolation. "An' I need them horses. I had a lot of money invested in them. They're necessary for the business. How could anyone do this?" Joe feared for a moment that the youngster was going to break down and cry.

"Oh, there's plenty folks in these parts who can do things like that easy enough. This is rough country. Ain'tcha found that out yet?" Joe's eye

22

rested for a few seconds on the smooth, uncalloused hands, then moved up to the beardless face, the soft mouth. A fish out of water, he thought. "Drink up," he said. "You'll feel better in a coupla minutes."

The young man sat without moving. "I was goin' to build a freight business." He spoke quietly, a man in shock and near despair. "Figgered I'd start with the mules, build the business up. I saw the opportunity there in Buckshot. There was freight bein' brought in from back East but nobody haulin' it out to the settlers an' miners."

"Yeah, you tol' me last night," said Joe. He leaned forward and tipped more whisky into the youngster's coffee can. He looked regretfully at the dwindling amount of liquid in the bottle. "You told me 'bout how you was goin' to Californy but got stuck in Buckshot when your wife got sick . . . an' 'bout how you saw the opportunity an' sold your wagon an' team to buy the mules an' saddle horses."

"I figgered I could build a business for myself an' my wife." The young man was speaking almost to himself. "She didn't want me to do it. Wanted me to go to California an' be a store clerk, like I had been in Council Bluffs, 'way back in Missouri. 'You could open your own store in California, in time', she kept tellin' me. 'You ain't the type to live in this wild country. Face it, Jim', she would say, 'you ain't the type. You're a city man'. But I wouldn't listen."

Old Joe nodded in unconscious agreement. "Maybe she was right, son? You thought about that? This is rough country, an' it ain't ever'body who . . . " He stopped awkwardly. He wanted to say 'She's right, son. You ain't the type. You're decent an' soft an'way too innocent to live out here. This land'll eat you up, destroy you. Better go back to Buckshot. Get your wife an' all your stuff and head for Californy, like she says. Be a store clerk. You were born for it.'

24

But he didn't dare say it. He sensed that remarks like that would destroy the youngster completely. He might even collapse right there in front of him, and then what would he do? Instead he said, "Let's round up your mules an' get your stuff loaded."

Later, the packs redistributed among the mules and the young man mounted on the strongest animal, old Joe took farewell of him.

"Take my advice, son," he risked saying. "An' that of your wife too. Get out to Cal'forny. It's better country there."

Jim Parry's next remark shocked the old miner. Parry shook his head. "No. Thanks all the same, Joe," he said, and there was a stubborn jut to his jaw, although his face was white and doleful. "I saw an opportunity in Buckshot; I know that opportunity is there, an' I'm gonna take it. I got to find the men who took my horses. I got to get them back. It ain't right that they should do this." He looked straight into the old miner's eyes. "I'm gonna find the men who took my animals. An' I'm gonna take them back."

Old Joe stood watching as the mule train stumbled back down the uneven trail. He was shaking his head in disbelief and dismay. "Son," he said to himself, half under his breath, "I reckon you're a mite too mule-headed for your own good. You jus' don' know the kind of men you're dealin' with out here. You go lookin' for those men, you liable to find them — an' then you'll be a lamb goin' to the slaughter."

2

Hannah Parry rose from the chair she was sitting in and took a deep breath. "Well," she said, "they're gone. One hundred and ten dollars' worth of horses. That's money, that is. That's a lot of money, for us." She shook her head sadly from side to side. "I hate to think of what we could have done with that money in California. But they're gone, and bad luck go with them." She turned towards her husband who was sitting slumped in a chair by the fire. "But we'll get over it. 'Into each life some rain must fall', as folks say. It's a heavy blow, but it isn't the end of the world. And at least we know what we have to do now."

Jim Parry looked up at her, his face pale, the corners of his mouth turned down. "You mean . . . "

"I mean we sell those mules, scrape

up what money we can, buy a wagon and team and get out to California. We can get a light wagon and a two-horse team. We'll get there, if we aren't in too much hurry. And when we get there my brother will help us."

She began pacing the room, thinking aloud, a trim, shapely young woman dressed a little too finely for a frontier town, a woman used to planning and to getting her own way. A shrewd observer might have thought that Jim Parry had married above himself and that it was his wife who wore the pants in that house. She stopped her pacing and turned again to her husband, her tone and attitude positive, resolved.

"Things will be tough for a while but we'll live. And we'll get on, I know we will. You can go to work for Phil, as a store clerk. You know he offered you a job already. And I can maybe get a little work, washing and cleaning maybe. I don't mind what I do — as long as I know that we're going places and not fooling about with . . . what? What do you mean? Why are you shaking your head like that?" She was staring at her husband, a puzzled frown on her face.

Jim Parry didn't get up. He stayed leaning forward in his chair, his forearms on his knees, but he continued to shake his head slowly.

His wife knelt down beside him in alarm. "Now look, Jim . . . " Her voice was strained, as though temper was about to break through disciplined calm.

"I'm gonna get those horses back." Parry's voice was a dull monotone. "I ain't leavin' here. I got to get them back. Like you said, there's more'n a hundred bucks invested in them animals. An' I'm gonna get them back. 'Sides, it ain't right that somebody should steal our horses. It just ain't *right*."

Hannah Parry stood up in near-speechless exasperation. "Lord give me strength!" she prayed. "It ain't *right*? It ain't *right*?" Her voice rose in raw anger. "When did right ever mean anything in this God-awful country? I've been telling you for months! This country is a desert, a wilderness. And the people are trash!" She stopped suddenly, biting her lip. Besides a good figure, a strong will and an education acquired in Miss Adelaide Remburgh's Academy for Young Ladies, in Saint Louis, Hannah Parry had a conscience and a regard for truth. "No. That's not true," she admitted. "I shouldn't have said that. No doubt some of them are decent people, but half of them have no initiative; they're content to stay here and just take what comes along, don't try to better themselves. And the other half are delinquents — crooks, thieves and ruffians. It's a Godless, lawless land and I wish I'd never set eyes on it. Let's get out of it and get on our way to California. It's civilized there, they *have* right and wrong, law and order! When we're there you can talk about . . . "

"I ain't goin'." Parry stood up. His

sunken shoulders and hanging head emphasized his natural thinness and his face was still pale but his jaw jutted out, the only firm thing about him. "We need those horses." Even his voice was weak. "Truth is, we ain't got enough money to fit out a new team an' wagon. An' I ain't gonna be beholden to your brother, or nobody else. An' them animals is mine. I saw a chance to make somethin' of myself here, in Buckshot, Montana, an' that chance was a real one; it still is. But I need those horses. An' I'm goin' to get them back. They can't be too far away. Horses can't fly."

His wife stood looking at him. "*You're* going to get them back?" She regarded him with disbelief and despair. "The sheriff says he can't do anything. You've no idea where they are; you've never had to do anything like this before; you don't know the kind of people you'd be dealing with. Jim Parry, you are the most mule-headed man that ever lived . . . " She almost ran out of breath and her temper finally broke through. "For God's sake, Jim," she yelled, "be sensible! You don't even know where to start looking!"

"I'm gonna get them back," the weak voice insisted. Parry looked at his wife in mute appeal. "We can't *afford* to jus' let them go," he pleaded. "I *got* to get them I jus' *got* to." He moved to the door. "As for where to start lookin' . . . I got to start from where I'm at. I'll start right here."

His wife threw up her hands in speechless indignation.

Parry left the house and drifted aimlessly down into town. Buckshot was a fair-sized place, as towns went, west of the Missouri. It boasted five different streets running in five different directions, nine saloons, four livery stables, five general stores and a rash of small businesses — saddlers, blacksmiths, feed and grain merchants and ironmongers — plus a barber-cum-dentist and a laundry. Parry drifted till he found himself outside the sheriff's office and, finding himself there, he went in.

Ward Gateley, the deputy, was standing by the desk, riffling his way through a pile of papers. A lean, fit man of around thirty with a well-worn shellbelt round his middle and a bone-handled Colt showing out of the holster. He looked up, a sheaf of papers held in one hand. "Yeah? What can I do for you?" He wondered for a moment what this spindly, pale-faced character was doing in a town like Buckshot. Just a pilgrim, he decided, passing through.

"It's about a horse." Even the voice was weak, Gateley thought. "Well, a couple of horses. Stolen. I been in to see Sheriff Houghton already. I jus' wondered . . . " Parry stopped and shrugged his shoulders. "I mean, if there was anything."

"You know who stole them? These horses?" Gateley's attention went back to the pile of papers on the desk. Work was piling up. There'd been a killing a few miles out of town, an armed hold-up over by Bitter Creek and an outbreak of what might be smallpox among some pilgrims approaching the town in a wagon train. He'd also been warned that some rough characters were heading towards Buckshot. And just when Sheriff Houghton's lumbago was bad, so that he had to go home and lie down for lengthy periods. Gateley had more than he could handle right now: Stolen horses he could do without.

"No. I don't know who coulda stole them." Parry shook his head miserably.

"Where was they stolen? Here in town?"

"No. 'Bout fourteen miles away. In the foothills. Out by Wild River."

"When was this?"

"Four days ago."

"Why didn't you report it before?"

"I did. Tol' Sheriff Houghton soon as I got back. I ain't been back long. I had deliveries to make. I run a mule train. They was my saddle animals."

"An' you got no idea who mighta stole them?"

Parry shrugged. "No."

Gateley looked up from his papers and sighed. "What did Sheriff Houghton say?"

"He said if I hadn' no idea who stole them he couldn' do much. Said the animals could be anywhere. Anywhere in the whole country."

"He take a description of the animals?"

"Yeah. A buckskin an' a bay. Both geldin's. Both around fifteen hands, or jus' short."

Gateley shrugged. "Sheriff's right. Unless you got some idea who took them, or where they might be, there ain't much we can do. We'll keep an eye open but I wouldn' expect too much, if I was you." He frowned and shook his head in annoyance. "We can't go aroun' lookin' at every horse in the territory. It'd be like lookin' for a needle in a goddamn haystack."

Parry nodded hopelessly. "Yeah. That's what the sheriff said." He shuffled towards the door.

"You goin' West?" Gateley asked, slightly curious. "Goin' to Oregon, or Cal'forny?"

"Was goin' to Cal'forny." The man still held his head low. "But I figgered I'd start a freight comp'ny here, in Buckshot. I got the mules. But no horses now."

Gateley hesitated. He didn't believe in giving advice but he could do without this man's problems. Better if he just went away. "I think if I was you I'd go right on to Cal'forny," he said. "Things is better there. This ain't no place for a new man to start a business. Too goddamn rough. If I was you I'd take my mules an' go to Cal'forny. You'd have a better chance there."

The man nodded weakly and continued on his way to the door. Gateley wasn't sure if he had heard him or taken in what he had said. He didn't seem to be hearing right. Gateley went back to more pressing problems.

Parry drifted around aimlessly and found himself back at the yard where he corralled his mules. He stood for a few minutes looking blankly at them through the rails.

"They all right, mistuh? Yo' animals, Ah mean."

Parry looked up to see a lean, elderly Negro leaning on a stable broom beside him. He'd seen the man before — he worked in the livery stable, wore an old suit of overalls over his bare, mahogany-coloured torso, the crotch hanging halfway to his knees, his crinkly hair grey as the ashes of a camp-fire. He had a strange name too, nickname no doubt . . . Drag something . . . yeah! Slowdrag, that's what they called him, Slowdrag. Parry looked at him. "Yeah, the mules are all right," he mumbled.

"'Cause if you wants them fed extry — or if you wants somebody to look at their feet. Ol' Slowdrag'll be glad to . . . "

"Naw." Parry shook his head miserably. "Naw. They're all right. Say, Slowdrag." He didn't know what he was saying or why he was saying it but just let the words come out. "You been aroun' this town a long time, ain'tcha? An' aroun' horses an' stables?"

"Sho' have." The old Negro grinned and reached down behind his collar to scratch his bare back. "Slowdrag been hoss-keepin' mos' of his life. Here, an' in other places too. Horses, mules, burros. Done a little horsebreakin', when Ah was younger. Ah kin shoe, an' doctor some too."

"You ever had horses stolen? Or known 'bout stolen horses."

The old Negro shook his head slowly from side to side. "Ah ain't nevah had a horse stole. But Ah ain't nevah had no horse of mah own to *git* stole. But Ah heard of animals that got stole, time to time. It's a bad business, stealin' horses." The old voice rose and fell in a musical sing-song. "Steal a man's horse, you kinda take away half his life. On'y a bad man'll do that kinda thing — but they's plenty bad men aroun'." He shook his grey head again, slowly and solemnly.

"You think there's men in this town who'd steal a man's horse?"

The old Negro looked at Parry uneasily. "They's bad men in this town, like any other, mistuh." The whites of his eyes showed.

"Would you know where to find them? Here? In this town?"

The old man ceased to lean on the stable broom. He recommenced that slow shaking of the head, distinctly uneasy, and began to move away a little, his eyes going, almost involuntarily towards the north side of town. "Like Ah was sayin', mistuh, they's bad men in ever' town. This'n ain't no different." Specially up that end." His white-eyed glance went once more to the north end of Buckshot. He seemed to have second thoughts and turned away rather abruptly. "But Ah ain't sayin' nothin'. Ah ain't had no horses stole, is all Ah know." He took himself off, half-plying his broom in rhythmic sweeps.

Parry found himself moving towards

the north end of town, not sure of what he was going to do or why. The area didn't look any different from the other areas of town: a few eating-houses, store or two, some tar-paper shacks where people lived, stables here and there. It wasn't any less respectable than any other area in any other town.

He stopped outside a long building with a sign saying 'Eagle Livery, J. Hinds, Prop.' The door was open. Inside he could see long lines of stalls. The sounds of horses chomping and stamping came to his ears. Parry edged his way in. "Hello!" he called. "Anybody there?" No one answered.

There were seven horses down one side, nine down the other. Mostly saddle horses but with two or three heavier draught animals. Parry called again and still no one answered. He began to walk down the lines, looking closely at the animals in the stalls. Chestnuts, a steeldust, three greys and a black . . . two – three bays but these were draught animals, a couple of buckskins. He looked closely at these but neither of them looked like his, as far as he could see. They were short, quarter-horses, about fourteen-two hands. No, not his.

"You lookin' for somethin', mister?" A man had materialized behind him, a tall, lean man in dirty work clothes. There was a note of suspicion and annoyance in his voice. "You got a horse here?"

Parry felt distinctly uncomfortable. "Eh . . . no . . . no, I ain't. I was jus' . . . lookin'. I got some mules," he said, as inspiration came to his aid. He hated lying but he had to say something. "Wondered how much you'd take to look after them." The lean man was regarding him with open suspicion. "I called out but nobody answered."

The thin man studied him with open hostility. It was easy to be tough with an obvious weakling. "We ain't got room for no more stock," he said abruptly. "So get on your way." He

41

stood close, watching and waiting, half-hoping the fella might put up some resistance.

There was none. The fella nodded, mumbled something incomprehensible and slunk out, shoulders stooped, head hanging like a beaten cur. The stableman snorted contemptuously, feeling good in himself, and went back to the card game he had going in the loft.

3

Parry went on up the street and down another and along one more. He looked in every stable doorway. If nobody was around he went in and took an apprehensive look around. In one he tried the excuse that he was looking for someplace to stable his mules but the stable buck kept him at the door while he talked. There were no horses in the place anyway, he could see that much from the door.

The area that he was in now didn't seem the kind of place where stolen animals might turn up. It was beginning to look like the better part of Buckshot and it got even better as he went along. The stores were stone-built now, the houses more permanent, of wood and stone, the animals in the stables of a higher quality. People who lived like this didn't need to steal horses. He gave up the idea that he had any chance of finding his animals there.

He stopped outside a decidedly high-class place. In the corral to one side there were half a dozen prime animals, saddle horses all and of top quality. He eyed them sadly. A smart grey mare, pretty as a picture, a lady's horse for sure; two neat chestnuts, matched pair, for somebody's carriage; a big black with white blaze and feet, a smaller black, with a star instead of a blaze, a light, fast-looking steeldust. Whoever used this place had money. And people with money didn't need to steal horses.

More out of curiosity than hope, Parry eased his way through the open stable door. Again he called and again nobody answered. He moved quietly up the main stable, admiring the animals in the stalls on each side.

A buckskin, but too tall to be his . . . a classy little palomino, pretty as a showgirl with its cream mane and tail, two or three bays, but clearly branded and none of them his anyway. He'd know his bay — well, he hoped he would: he hadn't had his horses very long and inside himself he had to admit that one bay could look pretty much like another. But he *hoped* he would recognize it. There was a black stallion in the next stall then another buckskin, just about the height of his, two greys, one very light, the other dappled.

There was nobody around. Parry called again. Still no answer. He went into the buckskin's stall. He was trembling.

It was his horse. He knew it. "Scout!" he said. The horse showed no recognition. But he knew it was Scout. He *knew* it, the way you'd know your brother if you saw him, even in a crowd. And the horse wasn't bothered by him, the way he might be bothered by a stranger. It was Scout all right! Parry's heart was beating furiously. Maybe he was wrong? Maybe he was clutching at straws? Maybe it wasn't Scout? He shoved the horse to one side of the stall and examined the offhand quarter. Yes! There was the brand! The double 'A'. The mark of Andy Armstrong, Honest Andy, as he called himself, the horse trader he'd bought both of his animals from over at Bitter Creek as the dealer was passing through on a selling trip.

He bent down to pick up one of its feet. The lower leg wasn't darker than the upper. His heart sank like a stone. On Scout the buckskin shaded to brown below the knee. But it *was* Scout! He goddamn well *knew* it was him! He began to move around the animal, looking for other marks of confirmation. He took the horse's head, opened the mouth.

"Well, well, well! Whatta we got here?"

A voice drawled the words, lazily and pleasantly.

A man had come in noiselessly and was standing watching him, legs splayed apart. Tallish, lean, his face was sunburned red except for where a fearsome scar stood out white. His

46

dirty-blond hair was long, but not long enough to conceal the fact that the top of one ear was missing. He said nothing more for a minute then turned and called, "Brandy? Hey! Brandy! Come an' see what I've got." He stood grinning, hands by his side, legs splayed wide.

Parry stood up straight, wiping his hands on his thighs. "I ain't doin' no harm." His voice shook slightly. "Was thinkin' of buyin' a horse. Jus' lookin' . . . " He tried a weak smile.

The blond man said nothing. He stood just outside the stall, blocking Parry's exit. Another man came stomping in. A heavy man of around thirty, solid and hard, in worn town-clothes and scuffed cowboy boots, he moved like a man on his way to a fight.

"Whatcha got?" He slowed his pace when he saw that there was a man in the stall beside the buckskin, paused for a moment then moved right up and stood with one hand on the wooden stall wall. "Well! We got a buyer?"

Parry knew from the tone of the voice and the physical stance that there was trouble coming — bad trouble.

"He don't look like no buyer to me," the scar-faced man said. "Come outa there!" he ordered Parry. He glanced at his companion. "Know what? He looks like a horse thief to me. A goddamn horse thief." The men grinned at each other as if enjoying some private joke.

Parry tried a weak bluff. "I'm thinkin' of buyin' a horse," he said, putting all the confidence he had into his voice and it wasn't much. "Thought this'n looked good." He nodded at the buckskin as he came out of the stall.

"Where's your money? Show us your money." The thick, heavy man blocked his path, his expression changed to a sullen scowl.

"I . . . I didn't bring money with me. Not right now. Was jus' lookin'. But I got it all . . ."

"You seen this fella before, Jack?" The heavy man looked at his companion. He moved very close to Parry and

48

stared into his eyes. "Seems to me I seen him somewhere. Pokin' aroun' horses."

"I tell ya I'm thinkin' . . . " The breath went out of Parry as a fist like a sledgehammer-head pistoned into his belly. He doubled up in anguish, the world swimming before his eyes, and he stayed doubled up, submerged in a sea of pain and nausea. For a moment or two he was hardly conscious, then he knew he was on all fours on the cobbled floor of the stable, looking at dirty straw and feeling as if he was being disembowled. A hand grabbed him by the hair and he was hauled semi-upright, crying and gasping for air. Every step a crucifixion, he found himself shoved and dragged along. He was being hauled, manhandled, half-carried up a wooden stair. They were facing a polished wooden door. The heavy man held him and the one with half an ear knocked. The door opened and he was hauled inside.

Parry was still crying and gulping for

air. He could not stand and was held upright by the powerful, thick arms.

"Yeah? Who's this?"

A man had got up from behind a desk. He was about forty, well dressed in city clothes. A gentleman, no doubt about it. White shirt with starched collar and dark-blue silk tie, expensive dark suit, hand-made boots, a gold watch chain across his trim middle, gold ring on one finger. His hair was cut in a carefully conservative style, the neat little moustache underlining his respectability. The face under the thick curly mane was open and tanned, the face of decent authority, the face of a man of position and respectability.

"Found him below, pokin' around. He was in one of the stalls. Foolin' around, with that little buckskin." The heavy man spoke.

"You know him?" The city-dressed man came round from behind his desk and stood in front of Parry. He stood a few feet away, as if he might somehow become contaminated, either by Parry or by the men who held him. His expression was one of detached superiority and mild distaste.

"Yeah." It was the knife-scarred man who spoke this time. "We know him, Mister Samuels. We've seen him around that buckskin before." There was a curious inflection to his voice.

The man called Samuels looked quickly at the speaker. "Him?" The word carried a lot of meaning.

"Yeah. Him."

Samuels looked at the heavy man who held Parry by the arm and by the hair. "You too, Brandy? You know him?" His voice matched his appearance, a deep, well-modulated baritone. It might have been a politician or a lawyer speaking.

"It's him aw'right." Brandy Lee hauled Parry's head mercilessly back as though to present his face to Samuels' gaze.

Samuels moved half a step closer to Parry. "What are you doing here?"

"I'm lookin' for a horse." Parry

51

could hardly get the words out. They came out as gasps and groans.

"What did he say?" Samuels looked at Lee.

"Said he was lookin' for a horse."

Samuels gave the briefest of nods then turned back to his desk. He picked up a cigar from an open box, bit off the end and spat it out, a gesture not quite in keeping with his gentlemanly appearance. He lit the cigar from a sulphur match, drew on it for a minute then held it out and looked at it thoughtfully, blowing out a fragrant cloud of smoke. He turned back towards Parry, who was still heaving and retching in the iron grasp of the two men. He gave a little sigh of patient weariness and leaned forward so that his face was only inches from Parry's.

"Don't look for horses around here," he said. "Unless of course you've come to buy?" He glanced at Brandy Lee, his eyebrows raised in question.

"He ain't buyin'," Lee grinned. "I

tried him. Ain't got no money." His grin widened further. "'Sides, he couldn't afford a classy animal like that buckskin." Jack Holt sniggered along with him.

Samuels nodded, drew on his cigar and addressed Parry again. "Understand this: I run a respectable business. I've got a position to keep up in this town and I mean to maintain it. I resent any suggestion that there might be stolen horses on my premises. And I don't like casual strangers coming uninvited into my stables, interfering with my animals. You could be a crazy character, a fire-raiser, a horse-maimer . . . "

Parry struggled to get words out. "I wasn't doin' nothin' wrong. I wouldn't do nothin' like . . . "

"Shut him up!" Samuels spoke with polite weariness and Jack Holt stepped round and drove a massive fist into Parry's belly. There was a bad, frightening sound and Parry's voice stopped in mid-sentence: he was absolutely silent for several seconds.

Samuels stepped back half a pace and drew on his cigar, watching Parry heave and drool, almost insensible. He waited half a minute then stepped forward again and spoke close to Parry's face.

"I don't want to see you here again. I've got capable men here, looking after my property, and if you come poking around here again you'll find you've bitten off more than you can chew. Do you understand me?"

Parry hung limp, semi-conscious. He made no response.

"I said do you understand me?" The cultured voice took on a hard, vicious edge and old acne scars stood out on the tanned face, giving it an expression of suppressed savagery.

Parry's voice was a breathless whimper, "Yeah . . . yeah . . . I heard."

Samuels gestured with the hand holding the cigar. "Throw him out," he said. "But give him some first. Just to make sure he remembers."

The knife-scarred man sprang into

position in front of Parry. "Hold him up," he instructed with relish. Lee hauled Parry's head back and tightened his grip. The man drew back a fist and measured his distance with his eye.

"Not in the goddamn face!" snarled Samuels, glancing back towards them. "Not where it will show."

Again a fearsome piston-blow drove into Parry's belly, then another, and another. He dropped like a stone and Lee could not hold him. He was hauled up and held up again and this time the knife-scarred man was holding him. Brandy Lee was behind him. Lee began a series of terrible near-killing punches to his kidneys but Parry was unconscious and couldn't feel anything any more.

4

Reuben Wiles hauled on the reins and drew his elderly pair of bays to a halt, the brake on his old wagon screeching in complaint. Reuben swore softly under his breath. It wasn't like the dog to go off like that, especially so close to town: he knew he was needed there. Reuben liked to have the dog stand in the wagon while he organized the rest of his supplies. Chief was a good guard dog, rough-looking and with a convincing snarl and people were usually only too willing to give him a wide berth, which made Reuben feel better as he went from store to store. And now the goddamn critter had run off somewhere. Reuben swore again. The day was damp and his rheumatism troubled him. Now he'd have to walk back some distance and call him. Goddamn mutt!

He dismounted stiffly from the driving bench and tied the halter rope loosely to a sapling at the roadside. The bays began to snatch gratefully at the reachable grass and bushes. Reuben started to hobble back along the trail. Maybe chasing rabbits, he thought, but he didn't convince himself: Chief knew better than that. He plodded on, calling as he went and cursing between calls.

He had to trail back a couple of hundred yards before he heard the barking and then he had to leave the trail and beat around in the brush before he finally located the dog.

He was pulling at something lying in the bushes, pawing and scratching then looking around and barking excitedly, clearly worked up about something. "It ain't a rabbit," Reuben muttered to himself. "You know how much a rabbit's worth an' you don't get that worked up over one."

The barking grew more intense when the dog saw Reuben. "Aw'right, aw'right!" the old man soothed him.

"What you got there? Deer calf? Mite too big for you, huh? Wouldn't be a cougar, this close to town." He stopped suddenly. There was a man lying there. He looked dead. Reuben suddenly felt cold. Last thing you wanted to run into on your way into town was a death, however it might have happened.

He went forward gingerly. No blood around. It was a young man, and the face was unmarked, except that it was screwed up with pain. His own face screwed up with distaste, Reuben knelt down and touched the still face.

Warm. So he was still alive! Reuben felt for a pulse in the neck, under the ear, noting as he did so that the man's clothes were good, and nearly new, and he had his boots on. So he hadn't been robbed and he wasn't a bum. There was a pulse, too, medium strong. Reuben stood up. "Stay!" he told the dog and the dog almost nodded, having anticipated the command. "I gotta go back there an' git the wagon." He brushed his way through the undergrowth and back to the trail then began hobbling back as fast as he could, almost forgetting his pain in his anxiety.

★ ★ ★

"Where'd you say you found him?" Ward Gateley asked Reuben as between them they carried the body into the sheriff's office.

"Jes' 'bout quarter-mile outside town, on the north fork. Wasn't me that found him. Was the dog. He was lyin' in the brush, close to . . . "

"He's comin' round," said Gateley. The limp, helpless man had begun to moan. "Let's take him in there." Gateley nodded in the direction of the main cell. "Lay him on the bunk. Lucky we ain't got no other boarders right now."

They laid him out on the lumpy, straw-filled mattress.

"I know this fella," said Gateley, standing back and looking down at the inert figure. "He was in here jus' a little while ago. 'Bout a horse that was stole." He moved closer and pushed back the hair that had fallen over the man's face. "Yeah, it's him aw'right. Ain't nobody else like him in this town . . . skinny fella, new clothes. Yeah! It's him aw'right." He turned to old Reuben. "Say, Rube, would you stick around a li'l while an' mind the store? I oughta find out where this fella lives."

★ ★ ★

Ross Samuels pushed back his chair from his desk and studied the man standing, hat in hand, before him. Samuels spoke bluntly, the tanned face hard, uncompromising. "So what it boils down to is you can't pay me the money you owe me."

The man shuffled uncomfortably, twisting his worn stetson in his hand. His clothes were those of a rangeman, worn with long work, his calloused hands, leathered features and greying hair bearing testimony to a long life of toil with cattle in the open air. "It ain't that I can't pay, Mister Samuels." He struggled to find words, a man used to action rather than talk. "I can pay aw'right — if you give me a little time. It's jus' that right now . . ."

"I've already given you time. More than once."

"Yeah, I know. That's true. But at increased interest. That's part of the trouble, the interest. But I can come across. Only right now things ain't good. Cattle prices are down. If I can hang on a few weeks . . ." The man looked at Samuels, his elderly face grave, uncomfortable, a man not used to begging.

"You shouldn't be in business," said Samuels bluntly. "You buy several horses from me that you can't afford to pay for and can't afford to do without. That's not good management. And you expect me to subsidize you when you get into difficulties. That's unreasonable and I have every right to foreclose the deal." He studied the man in front of him again, weighing up just how much he might be worth and how far he could be pushed. "But I am not an unreasonable man. I'm prepared . . . " He snorted in annoyance as a knock sounded on the door. "Yeah? What is it?" The acne scars on his face stood out again as the latent anger in him rose almost to the surface.

The door opened and Jack Holt put his head around it. "Eh, boss — Mister Samuels," he corrected himself hurriedly, "Deputy Sheriff's here. Wants to see you."

Samuels' expression became neutral, revealing nothing. He looked at the rangeman. "I'll give you a month. Not a day longer, understand?" The rangeman nodded uncomfortably. "One month from today. No longer." He leaned back in his chair and put the tips of his fingers together. "The interest must go up to thirty per cent. And it will." His face showed a little emotion for the first time: just the faintest shade of pleasure and satisfaction.

"Thirty per cent!" The rangeman gasped. "But Mister Samuels! How can I . . . ?"

"Take it or leave it; said Samuels. "But do it now. Right now."

The rangeman shrugged and shook his head hopelessly. "Aw'right, Mister Samuels. I accept."

Samuels jerked his head towards the door, dismissing him. "Tell Deputy Gateley to come in," he called.

Gateley entered the room respectfully, his hat also in his hand. "Afternoon, Mister Samuels. Hope I ain't disturbin' you . . . business, I mean."

"No, Sheriff, it's all right. Take a seat." Samuels gave a hard smile and indicated the chair.

"It ain't much." Gateley sat on the edge of the cushioned seat and toyed with his hat. "Only I got a man down in the jail — well, that is I had him down there, he's back in his home now." He watched Samuels uncomfortably, hoping that Samuels might say something to help him. Samuels remained silent, his expression politely curious and sympathetic.

"Well," Gateley leaned forward, hands on his knees, and twisted his hat in his hands. "He says he was here, was lookin' at a horse kinda like one that he got stole . . . " Gateley took a deep breath. "An' he says that a couple of your men beat him up." His expression became almost apologetic. "I gotta look into it, Mister Samuels. An' Sheriff Houghton's outa action right now. Fact is we're . . . "

"It's all right, Sheriff." Samuels deliberately did not use the title 'Deputy'. "I understand. You have your job to do. And you do it well. It does you credit." He rose from the desk and moved to a drinks cabinet on the other side of the room. "A drink, Sheriff? I generally take a small one around this time." He held out a large shot glass.

Gateley flushed with pleasure. "Well, I shouldn' really, Mister Samuels, bein' as I'm workin'."

"Well, just this once." Samuels handed him a stiff shot of bourbon. He stood with his legs splayed apart, a drink in his own hand. "I'm afraid I know nothing about such an incident, Sheriff — oh! that's not to say it didn't happen!" He held up a hand to forestall any comment from Gateley. "It might have happened. I employ a number of men and — between ourselves" — he smiled confidentially at Gateley, — "some of them can be rough. They have to be, at times. Horse trading isn't for the soft and weak, I'm afraid."

Gateley looked uncomfortable. "The fella says this horse had his brand on it. A double 'A' brand."

Samuels looked thoughtful. "Double 'A'? Could easily be. I buy horses from Andy Armstrong, from time to time. That's his brand. 'Honest Andy' he calls himself. A travelling horse trader.

He supplies horses to lots of people in this territory. There must be many people with horses bearing that brand. But I assure you, Sheriff, I've got bills of sale for all of those animals . . . " He broke off and made to move towards his desk.

"That's OK, Mister Samuels." Gateley made a gesture of dismissal. "There ain't no need to . . . " He looked uncomfortable. "You understand Mister Samuels, I ain't sayin' . . . "

"No, but you're right, Sheriff." Samuels put up a hand again to reassure him. "It has to be investigated." He went to the door, opened it and called, "Jack? Come up here a minute, will you?"

There was a few seconds' delay then a clumping on the stairs and Jack Holt came in. He stood awkwardly in the centre of the room, straw and hayseeds clinging to his clothes. "Yeah, Mister Samuels? You wanted me?"

"Yes, Holt. Sheriff Gateley here has come to see me with a complaint.

Seems there was a man here. Looking at horses. Complains that he was beaten up?" He turned to Gateley. "When was this, Sheriff?"

"This mornin', Mister Samuels. Jus' today."

"Holt?" Samuels looked at Holt, his eyebrows raised.

"Yeah, well it was like we told you, Mister Samuels." Holt looked uncomfortable and sincere. "Brandy an' me. That fella did come in here. Was interferin' with a horse, little buckskin. He came in without no permission nor nothin'. When we asked him to leave he cut up rough. Took a swing at Brandy. 'Course Brandy took a swing back. You know Brandy. They swapped punches for a while then the fella ran off. That's all I know. Brandy got a closed eye." Holt tried an experimental smile. "He was real mad. Don't like to get bested in a fight."

Samuels nodded. "Yes. I remember now, you told me about that incident. I didn't realize it was that serious." He put on a very grave expression. "Tell Lee to come up here," he said. "I want to see him."

"Well, he ain't here right now," Holt's reply came almost too readily. "He rode over to Nine Wells, to collect them colts, like you said. Gonna be gone two – three days."

Samuels shook his head in mock exasperation. He glared at Holt. "How many times have I told you?" he said angrily. "I won't have my business the scene of a roughhouse? I run a respectable business and I have a reputation in this town. I won't have that reputation compromised. If there's any trouble it's the sheriff's job to attend to it." Angrily he paced up and down for a few seconds then turned to berate Holt again. "I've had to speak to you and Lee before," he barked, "about fighting. If you weren't good stablemen I'd fire you right here and now."

"I wasn't involved, Mister Samuels," Holt protested in an injured tone. "It was Brandy. An' the fella went for

68

him, like I said. Caught him on the eye. Woulda made any man mad." He looked at Gateley. "I mean, a fella goes for you, socks you on the eye, what you gonna do, huh?"

Samuels gestured to him to be silent then turned to Gateley. "This is awkward, Sheriff."

Gateley was on his feet. "It's OK, Mister Samuels. I reckon I know what happened. Maybe I'll talk to your man when he gets back. Right now I got a lot to attend to, Sheriff Houghton bein' off an' all that." He put his empty shot glass on the desk. "Thanks for the drink." He moved towards the door and stopped with one hand on the doorknob. "Tell your man, won'tcha? Go easy with his fists. Only makes more work for us. Can lead to trouble." He put on his stetson and gestured with his right hand, a half-salute. "Nice talkin' to ya, Mister Samuels. An' thanks again for the drink." He went out and clumped his way downstairs.

The two men in the room waited in

silence until the sound of his footsteps faded away then Samuels walked to the cabinet and replaced his shot glass. "He gone?" he asked Holt, who was looking out of the window. His voice had lost some of its refinement and sounded more natural.

"Yeah." The false, awkward sincerity was gone from Holt's voice too; his tone was familiar, with a slight note of contempt for Gateley. "He's gone to keep the law."

"You think he's satisfied?" Samuels walked to the window and stood beside Holt, watching Gateley's retreating back.

"Yeah." Holt's tone was derisory. "He's jus' dyin' to please."

Samuels went back to the drinks cabinet and poured himself another whisky, a large one. "You been overdoin' the rough stuff," he grunted.

"Hell!" Holt swore. "You said to . . ."

"Yeah, I know. But you got to know just how far to go."

"You wasn't always so partic'ler — in

the old days. You didn't mind handin' it out, either with your fists or with a gun or knife." Holt spoke familiarly, as though to an equal. "I can think of a few men you broke."

Samuels flexed the fingers of his right hand, low down by his side, as if remembering old gun-fighting skills. "Yeah. But that was the old days. I'm respectable now — and respectability pays. We've got a good racket goin' here and I don't have to do the rough work personally."

Holt studied him for a moment then said, "If folks knew what you was like before they'd be mighty glad of that."

Samuels grinned and the cultured, respectable face took on a brief expression of wickedness. He threw back half of his whisky. "Where's Brandy?"

"He's in the hay loft."

"Tell him to stay there till I send for him."

Holt grinned. "Won't be no problem.

He's got a woman up there — an' a bottle."

★ ★ ★

Jim Parry shook his head and turned away with a grimace of pain. "Naw, Hannah, I don't want no more. I can't eat right now."

His wife frowned and lowered the bowl of venison stew that she had been feeding him from. She looked at her husband as he half lay, half sat up in bed. "Just rest," she told him. "Maybe if you sleep a little you'll feel better."

"I don't need sleep. I ain't tired." Parry's face was pale and drawn but that stubborn chin of his stuck out as much as ever. "I need to get my horses back, that's all I need."

His wife knelt down by his bedside and took one of his hands in both her own, her expression very serious. "Jim," she pleaded, "listen to me. Please. Let's take all our stuff — everything we can carry — and get out of this town, this territory. We've still got the mules. We can sell some of them and buy a light wagon, and the remaining mules can pull it. Let's go to California. You can get a job there, as a store clerk. You're good at that. It's what you're cut out for, Jim. This . . . this . . . " She looked around her, stuck for words. "This wild, savage country isn't for you. The kind of people who live here, in this wilderness, they're not our kind of people. Jim, if you persist in this crazy idea of yours, well, I'm afraid you'll be hurt, hurt bad like you are now." She raised a hand and wiped away the start of a tear. She took a deep breath and composed herself again. "Jim, you could get yourself killed."

"OK, OK!" Parry hauled himself back off the pillows and leaned towards her, supporting himself on one forearm. "I been listenin', Hannah. An' what you say makes sense. But I got somethin' to say, too, an' it's important that you understand me."

He paused for a moment as though

to find the words he needed. "I saw a chance for us in this town. Yeah! I know it's a rough town. All these trail towns are, wild an' rough. But they ain't always gonna be that way. They're jus' beginnin' their lives. One day they'll be grown-up towns, with lots of stores, an' schools an' doctors an' dentists an' a railway an' maybe a music hall an' high-toned families livin' here — folks who'll come a-callin' and folks that we'll visit."

"Yes, but Jim . . . "

"Naw, hold on a minute, Hannah. What I'm a-tryin' to say is that one day these towns'll be rich. An' the people who got into business in them will be rich too. It's the people who start in right at the beginnin' — they're the ones that have the chance to make somethin' of themselves. Now there's a great chance for a man to build a freight haulage business here. I *know* it, Hannah. I'm a storekeeper, like you jus' said. I can *feel* when there's a business opportunity. It's here, in

Buckshot, right here an' now. I gotta take it, Hannah. It might never come again. This might be my one big chance."

"But Jim!" Hannah Parry was desperate. "It's too rough for you. Starting in a place like this, among men like these. You ought to start in a place that's already settled."

Parry shook his head. "When a place is settled, Hannah, the business chances are settled too. Tradin' is already established an' them that was there first have got it all. An' there's another thing . . . " He swung his legs out of bed and rested his feet on the floor. "Somebody stole my horses. Out here that's like takin' away a man's life." He was thinking of what the Negro, Slowdrag, had said. "It's like as if a man had said to me: 'Jim Parry, you ain't gonna have no haulage business, no life, because I say so'." Parry looked earnestly at his wife's drawn face. "I can't have that, Hannah, can I? What kinda man would I be if I let another man take my life away from me? Why, I couldn't *live*, Hannah."

His wife had risen. She walked around a few paces, distraught. "Jim, Jim, what on earth are you proposing to do?"

"I ain't proposin', Hannah. I'm jus' gonna get them horses back."

He thrust back the crumpled bed covers and stood up shakily. He cut a poor figure, a thin, white-bodied man, half bent over, crouching defensively from the pain and hurt inside him. The memories of his beating came back vividly to him and he felt fear stir uneasily in his belly.

But he took a painful breath, gathered all his courage together in one small heap and stepped shakily forward to get his pants from the back of a chair.

5

That little heap of courage drained almost entirely away from Parry as he stood in the privy a few minutes later and realized he was pissing blood.

He stood watching the dark red stream falling away from him, unable to stop it, and felt cold fear clutch at his heart. His life blood was literally draining out of him.

He finished, buttoned up his pants and stood leaning weakly against the wooden wall of the little rickety shack.

Jesus! What was he going to do? Maybe he was going to die? He had no knowledge about medical matters, had no idea of what damage might have been done to his insides — but when a young, otherwise healthy man started pissing blood! Jesus! That was bad.

And what about Hannah? What about his wife? Suppose he died

and left her here in this goddamn hell-hole? What would happen? He stopped thinking because he daren't think any further.

Outside, he sat down with his back against the privy because he couldn't trust himself to walk. Maybe he was going to die here, in this place where he had hoped to make his fortune. His eyes rested on the flimsy home-built house that he had made for himself and his wife. It was half wood, half tar paper, had been a quarter-built shack that someone had abandoned and Parry had finished it off with tar paper. He'd had great ideas about how he would rebuild it properly when he'd made some money.

Made some money! He made a sound that was half a snort, half a sob. Made some money! And now he was likely to die.

He sat there for some time, lacking the strength to do anything else. He daren't go into the house because his wife would see there was something wrong. So he just sat there, afraid to move, afraid to think.

But man is a curious animal. It's hard to say how individual men might act when the chips are down: some become philosophical, some just give up the ghost. And some fight back.

When the worst of the fear had drained out of Jim Parry, anger began to take over, anger at the men who had done this to him, and along with anger came a growing determination to set the balance right. Back in Council Bluffs, Missouri, he hadn't been called Mule Head Parry for nothing.

"I ain't dead yet," he told himself, and immediately felt a little better. "It maybe ain't surprisin' that I'm pissin' blood. That fella hit me in the back, low down. Ain't that where the kidneys is? Maybe stands to reason that I'm hurt some — but I ain't dead. Not yet. An' I ain't gonna let them bastards do this to me." He rose, shakily, and started to make his way into town, back to that stable where he'd seen his horse.

"It *is* my goddamn horse," he swore to himself, "even if the lower legs are a different colour."

It was a long, painful journey and on the way his feelings fluctuated between anger and fear. The thought of that place and of what might await him there caused him to slow up from time to time while his anger sometimes spurred him on to try to go faster than he was able.

Halfway there he found he couldn't go on and he wouldn't go back, so he sat down where he was, close to the corral where his mules were kept. His back against a fence post, he waited for both his physical strength and his courage to come back to him.

"You OK, mistuh?" He looked up to see the Negro stable buck standing before him, a look of worried curiosity on his lined face. He had his long broom with him, looking as if it were part of him.

"Yeah," Parry sighed. "Yeah . . . I think I'm OK. I jus' gotta wait a little. Till I'm sort of all here, in one piece."

"You don't look too good, mistuh, you don't mind mah sayin' so." The Negro voice lilted musically in gentle sympathy.

"I'm OK. Thanks."

"It ain't nothin'." The Negro began to move away, plying the big stable broom with rhythmic sweeps as if it were some kind of primitive musical instrument.

"Say, Slowdrag." Parry didn't want to be left alone.

"Yassuh?" The rhythmic sweeping stopped. Slowdrag looked back at him.

"You know about horses. You ever heard of folks changin' a horse? I mean, changin' his appearance? Makin' him look like a different animal?"

Slowdrag came back a few lazy paces. "Hmmm!" He gave a kind of chuckle. "It wouldn't be the fust time. I guess some people been doin' that a long time. Long, long time." He chuckled again. "Folks been cheatin' with horses long as there's been people an' horses."

"Could they change a horse's colour? Well, part of his colour?"

"Ah ain't nevah seen it done, maself." The voice changed key, went up a tone, in keeping with the Negro's increased interest, "But Ah heard of it, plenty times. They usin' dyes to do it. Git the dyes from plants an' sichlike. Mah pappy tol' me 'bout it too. He was a stable buck, all his evah-lovin' life." The old Negro grinned in gentle reminiscence.

"Could they change an animal's lower legs? From brown to buckskin?"

"They sho' could. Tha's what they does. They don' try to change a whole horse, make a black horse white, no suh! They tries to change him jus' a li'l bit — like one foot maybe, or maybe a leg, coupla legs. Jus' dyes it a li'l lighter, maybe, or darker. Makes a horse look different."

"Slowdrag? You know of anybody around here might deal in stolen horses?" Parry watched the Negro's face carefully.

He didn't miss the look of fear. "Uhhh-uhhh." The old stable buck shook his head worriedly. "Ah don't ask no questions, mistuh. An' Ah don't go lookin' in no dark corners. Ah does mah job an' Ah takes mah money an' Ah goes home to mah woman. An' Ah wants to go on doin' jus' that."

Parry felt a sudden acute spasm of pain in his belly. He sucked in his breath, his face screwed up and his hands clutched his middle.

"You all right?" Slowdrag came a step closer. "Somebody been beatin' up on you, mistuh?"

"I'll be OK." Parry let his breath out in a sigh. "I had a horse stole. Coupla horses. I think they could be here in town. Up that way." He jerked his head northwards.

The stable buck leaned down to look intently into his face. "You bes' be careful, mistuh. They's some bad men up in that end o' town."

He understood Parry's questioning expression and his voice dropped to a hoarse whisper. "They works for that Samuels gennelman. They real bad. One got half an ear. Other one a heavy man, hard, hard man. Mean as a angry rattleshake. Ah ain't sayin' they steals horses, but they's talk. But Ah'd keep away from them. Horse ain't worth losin' yo' life for."

He shook his head again then turned and limped off, not swishing his broom this time and moving more quickly than he had done before.

Parry sat where he was for another ten minutes then heaved himself up and made his way back to the stable where he'd seen his horse. Although he wished it was otherwise he found that his fear increased the nearer he got to it. He had to stop once or twice on the short journey and it wasn't the pain in his belly that made him do so.

He stopped at the corner of the building, leaned against the wall, heart thudding frighteningly, and put his head round the corner.

The big door was standing open. Nobody around. Parry breathed deeply. Maybe those two men were inside? If he went in they'd grab him again. He'd never been a fighting man and right now he was in even poorer condition for it. His wife's words came back to him: 'Jim, you could get yourself killed'. That wasn't an exaggeration. He could be living his last few minutes right now. Maybe he would be wise to let it go, to turn around and go home and forget about his stolen horses? Maybe he should settle for staying alive? The truth was, he realized in a flash of insight, he *wanted* to turn around and go back home.

But something inside him told him that the way to go was forward, not back, and Parry edged round the corner, scanned the empty yard with his eyes and eased himself along the wall towards the open door.

There was no sound from inside.

He paused at the empty door. Still no sound. He put his head inside. Only the gloom of an empty stable. He took a few cautious steps forward. Then a few more.

Most of the stalls were empty now. A couple of old draught animals, a chestnut and a bay, were drowsing in the middle pair of stalls. The rest were empty, bare, swept out.

Parry moved carefully up to the end of the building. Perhaps there was another stable, a connecting door? He looked all over. There wasn't.

He came out of the building and quietly searched around. No trace of those quality animals. They'd all gone — the smart palomino, the steeldust, the two blacks, all gone. And the men had gone too. Parry examined himself to see whether he was relieved or disappointed and found that he was both.

He made his way back to the livery stable where his mules were kept. The Negro was sweeping in the yard.

He looked up, white-eyed, as Parry approached.

"Say, Slowdrag." Parry wasn't exactly sure of what he wanted from the Negro. He paused and let the words come to him. "You got any idea if the men who work up there" — he jerked his head backwards towards Samuels' place — "I mean the man with half an ear, an' the other one . . . you got any idea if they got another place . . . place where they keep horses."

The white eyes grew bigger and rounder in the mahogany-coloured face. "Ah don' know, mistuh. Like Ah said already, Ah jus' does mah job an' Ah takes mah money an' . . . "

"Yeah, yeah, I know." Parry fished in his pocket and brought out his billfold. He peeled off a couple of bucks and looked at them anxiously. He was in no position to be buying information; his savings were meagre and likely to dwindle even further in the near future. He held out the money. "Think, now. Didja ever hear of any place — kinda quiet place — where people might keep horses — a lotta horses?"

The Negro watched the bills in his hand, his face a mixture of longing and apprehension. "Uhuh, mistuh." He shook his head slowly, fear clearly winning the upper hand, "Ah don' take to do with no horses that ain't right here. Ah jus' . . . "

"Look, Slowdrag!" Parry added another two bucks and, in wild recklessness, another. "Five bucks for you. An' there ain't nobody gonna know you tol' me. Honest. That's a promise." He shoved the money forward another couple of inches.

The Negro eyed the money in wonder. It was a lot of money to him. That money could buy new shoes for him and his wife. His eyes dropped involuntarily to the broken boots on his feet. How was he going to replace them?

And it wasn't just the money. He liked this man, and the man had been beaten up. He seemed a good man, and it wasn't right. He shook his head slowly from side to side. "Ah ain't sayin' that nobody stole no horses, mistuh. Ah ain't sayin' that mind."

Parry offered the money again. "I know. I ain't askin' you to say anybody stole horses. I jus' wanna know, have you ever heard anythin' — workin' around the stables, I mean — 'bout a place where lots of horses might be kept?"

Slowdrag swished his broom and looked at the ground. "Ah've heard folks say, time to time — an' they didn't say it out loud — would say it kinda quiet-like — that there is a li'l canyon, 'way out of town, between Nine Wells an' here an' that sometimes they's some prime animals grazin' there. Real fancy stock, ladies' mounts an' high-class saddle stock."

Parry nodded, his suspicions confirmed. "Thanks, Slowdrag." He held out the money.

"No suh." Slowdrag shook his grey woolly head. "I ain't tellin' you fo' the money. Ah jus' . . . "

"Take it, an' welcome. An' don't think I'll mention this to nobody. I won't." Parry forced the money into the brown, calloused hand.

"Why thank yo' kin'ly, mistuh." The Negro began to move slowly away, swishing his broom, then he turned and looked back at Parry. "Ah think that canyon might be somewhere 'round Eagle Ford. But it ain't easy to find, Ah guess."

6

Brandy Lee and Jack Holt and two other men sprawled on the ground around a fire, smoking and drinking from a bottle that went round slowly and erratically.

"You think that bottle could find its way over this side now an' again?" One man, tall and lean, raised himself on his elbow and looked across the fire to where Jack Holt was nursing the whiskey. He caught Holt's eye and put a weak grin on his face, trying to make his remark a half-joke.

"Maybe," Holt drawled with deliberate slowness. "An' maybe not." He took a long deliberate pull at the bottle and passed it back in the reverse direction.

"You're supposed to be workin', Jake Wilson." Brandy Lee reached up a hand and took the bottle intended for him. "You oughta be out there ridin' herd on them horses. Sammy gonna be angry if anythin' happens to any of them animals."

"Shit!" Wilson spat in disgust. "Nothin' gonna happen, out here. Who in hell's out here? Ain't nobody even knows of this place."

"Maybe we oughta go, Jake." Another man spoke uneasily. "Mister Samuels said we gotta take care." He got to his knees and began dusting himself down.

"Coober's right," grinned Holt. His expression was one of keen enjoyment. "It's your turn. An' the boss said to take real good care of his animals."

Jake Wilson half rose. "Aw, yeah! Tonight we gotta take real good care. But las' night it was different. We was all lyin' drinkin' las' night. But then it was my goddamn whiskey we was drinkin' so that was all right. But tonight *I* gotta take real good care — because it's your whiskey we're drinkin' — or *you're* drinkin', you an' your friend." He glared across the fire at Holt and Lee.

"You lookin' for trouble, Jake?" Holt reached back and took the bottle from Lee again. He took another pull at it and handed it back. "'Cause if you are . . . " He stood up lazily, hitched up his pants and took one step towards Wilson. His expression was one of quarrelsome enjoyment.

"You know that ain't . . . " Wilson stalled, aware that he might have gone too far. "I was jus' sayin' . . . "

"Aw, leave him go, Jack," Brandy Lee drawled from his position on the ground. "The shithead ain't worth it. Have another drink." He held the bottle aloft. "An' you, shithead" — he nodded towards Wilson — "git yore ass in the saddle an' ride around those animals till I come an' tell you you can stop. You an' your li'l boy here." He nodded in the direction of the other man already on his feet.

Wilson stood for a minute, saying nothing. Holt watched him, eye to eye, hoping he might resist further.

"Come on, Jake!" The man named Coober moved away from the fire a couple of feet, trying to draw Wilson with him. "We're nighthawkin'. We oughta be out there. You know what Samuels is like." He clearly wanted to avoid trouble with Holt and Lee. "Come on, let's go."

"Naw, naw!" drawled Holt, brushing aside Coober's remarks. "Let him stay. Maybe he got somethin' he wants to do. Eh, Jake? You think maybe you oughta do somethin'?"

"Aw, shit! Come on!" Jake Wilson capitulated, lowering his head and shoulders and turning away from Holt. Spitting with suppressed anger and frustration he followed Coober to where their horses were tied.

"Best leave them two alone," muttered Coober as the pair rode off into the darkening evening. "You know what they're like, 'specially when they been drinkin'."

"You think I'm scared of One-Ear?"

Wilson swung round angrily in his saddle. "Or his friend Lee? Shit! You don't know me, cowboy! I got a good mind to . . . " He hauled savagely on his bridle, dragging his horse round.

"Naw! Leave it, Jake!" Coober put out a hand to stay him.

"Think I'm chickenshit?" snarled Wilson. Coober was smaller, less hard than Holt or Lee. Wilson could deal with Coober. "If you think I'm scared, get down off that goddamn horse an' I'll . . . "

"Naw! I ain't sayin' you're scared." Coober shook his head, drawing his mount backwards. "I'm jus' sayin' them fellas is best left alone. They ain't worth gittin' killed."

"You better not." Wilson hauled on his bridle again, taking his wrath out on his horse. "Anybody thinks I'm scared . . . " He spurred his animal unnecessarily and rode away from Coober, mouthing obscenities and spoiling for trouble.

★ ★ ★

Jim Parry moved quietly amongst the grazing herd, stopping here and there to study a particular animal. There were thirty or forty in all and he had already spotted the palomino mare he had seen in Samuels' stable so he was sure there was some tie-up between the two places. It hadn't been easy finding the valley, even though he'd been looking for it and had some idea where it was. Certainly the woods that surrounded it would keep it hidden from people just passing by.

Parry stopped and looked around him. These were all good animals, high-class stock, and well broke. They didn't shy away from him as half-wild cow ponies would, but stood still and allowed themselves to be handled. But he hadn't seen his buckskin or bay yet.

He shoved quietly through a group of dark-coated animals. It would be hard to spot a particular bay in this dark.

There was a lighter-coloured horse grazing amongst them. He eased his way forward, his heart beginning to beat faster.

It could be Scout. The animal looked up and saw him and immediately lowered its head to graze again, unconcerned. Parry laid hands on it. It didn't mind.

Parry ran his hands all over it. It could be Scout. The mane had been trimmed close — and the tail — making it look different. He tried to determine the colour of the lower front legs but the night was too dark. "Scout," he whispered, watching to see if the animal showed any recognition.

Then he remembered. The man who had sold him the horse had told him of a trick the animal had learned: if you tapped him sharply on the rear legs, below the buttock, he would lie down. Parry drew a sharp breath. Now he would know for sure. He tapped the animal firmly, low down on the haunch. At that moment the group of animals grazing beside him scattered in a sudden drubbing of hoofs. A rider was blundering up straight in his direction. The buckskin horse was sinking, slowly, awkwardly settling down. "Hey! You!" someone shouted. Parry looked up and saw a dark-mounted figure almost upon him and not slowing down. Then he was falling and someone was on him, beating him, battering him and the buckskin horse was jumping up, anxious to be away from that scene of violence.

Fierce confusion. Half buried under a fierce, violent aggressive force. Hoofs thudding close — very close — to his head. Another inch and his brains would be . . . He jerked his knee up without knowing he was doing it. Smell of horses, feel of damp grass and a body trying to destroy him. Something very hard — a boot — hit him on the cheek. Thinking he was going to die.

He'd never been in a fight before, never in his whole life. Didn't know how. Didn't know what to do.

But he was on his feet and there was a man lunging at him intent on destroying him, a tall, lean man with lank, hanging hair and a bad smell.

Something else was new. Anger. A whole new different feeling. It filled Parry like a gas. He didn't want out of the fight now: he wanted into it. He sidestepped quickly, almost slipping on the damp grass, not knowing what to do and just letting instinct serve him. The dark body surged towards him again. Parry dropped like a shot deer and the body fell over him. He kicked out and felt his boot connect. He was on his feet again and kicked out again and again, connecting every time.

The figure was back on its feet. More wary now. Keeping a little distance from him and shouting as if to others nearby. It pulled at something round its waist. Parry threw himself forward without thought, without care, and felt his head connect with the man's jaw. Then they were on the ground again and Parry was on top.

The figure under him sluggish, hardly moving, but still warm. Mechanically, Parry drummed blows on its ribs and at its head. It took him several seconds to realize that the figure was no longer retaliating.

He was on his feet. Soft darkness surrounding him. Horses grazing some way off, far enough away to feel safe, to ignore the fight. Tall, thin form on the ground, crumpled up, still. Parry put his hand to his own face, felt his cheek. It went in where it should have stayed out. Something broken. Blood was flowing. His or the man's? Both? He was breathing like a steam engine. Anger filled him from head to toe. That figure on the ground had tried to kill him. He tried to think of what he ought to do next. There was sound from further off. A rider coming, maybe? Yeah! The sound was unmistakable, a drubbing of hoofs, and off aways, against the skyline he could see a galloping rider. He heard the call, "Jake? Jake? You there, Jake?"

Parry stood dazed for several seconds. The figure on the ground groaned and began to get to its feet. Parry stepped forward, bent down and lammed it on the jaw as hard as he could and then ran. Ran into the darkness, where it was thickest.

7

The three riders drew rein just outside Buckshot and peered at its main street from the shelter of a weedy bank. "Jus' another goddamn town," grunted one, standing in his stirrups and leaning forward as though to get a better view.

"An' what did you think it would be? Paradise?" the man alongside him sneered grumpily. All three were dirty and trail-worn, men who had been sleeping in their clothes for weeks. They were poorly mounted, on ageing, stiff-legged animals whose heads drooped and whose coats were coming out in tufts.

"It's called Buckshot," the third man drawled lazily. "Either of you ever been in it before?" He was lean and hard. Strange eyes, as yellow as a cat's, looked down over a broken nose and a beard like black barbed wire. He wore a shoulder holster over a grimy shirt and vest, the butt of a big pistol showing high under his arm. "Huh?" He kicked his rickety horse forward to bring himself alongside his companions. "Anybody been here before?"

"Don't think so, Ike." The first man spoke again. Another strange character. Heavy and fat, with a yellow moon face, the forehead and upper cheeks tattooed with some intricate blue design, the lower part fringed by a straggling dirty-blond beard. He wore deerskin shirt and pants, both garments blackly ingrained with dirt and body grease, like the tattered moccasins on his feet. He carried no firearm but a big knife stretched down his left thigh in a deerskin sheath. He glanced at the man called Ike. "Kinda hard to say. Livin' on the move — I mean." He shrugged. "Cain't always tell."

"I ain't never been here." The third man spat in disgust. "Ain't never been this far west." He was a solid, thick man, his face and neck burned red by the sun. Rat-coloured hair hung over his broad forehead and fringed his bull neck. His mouth had an odd twist to it, the result of a broken jaw that had not set properly.

"Well." The man called Ike leaned sideways in his saddle and spat into the dust. "It don't matter much. We got to go in anyways. Got to eat. Other things too." He grinned a hard, careless grin. "How much money we got?" He looked at the moonfaced, tattooed man. "Cloud? How much you got?"

"I told ya already, plenty times."

"Tell me again."

The fat man screwed down into a pants pocket and brought out a small handful of coins. "That's how much."

Ike Grivitch snorted gently. "We won't git in no trouble with that." He glanced at the other man. "Ratbite? How' bout you?"

Ratbite Wallis stared back. "Six bits."

Grivitch snorted again. "Gonna have

to sell a horse. Come on."

They pushed their shabby nags up towards the town.

Whitby Wells, owner of the Good Grass Livery Stable saw them coming and went into his shabby office for the derringer that lay in his battered desk. He slipped the wicked little weapon down the front of his overalls and went back out to meet them. "Howdy. What can I do for ya?" They were as hard a bunch as he'd seen in some time.

"You wanna buy a horse?" Ike Grivitch spoke, the other two hanging back behind him a little.

Whitby's eyes took in their animals. "Why?" he asked, trying a joke. "You know someone who's got one?"

Grivitch looked at his companions. "We got a comic here." There was some genuine amusement in his battered face. He indicated Ratbite Wallis's mount. "You can have him for ten bucks."

Whitby Wells shook his head. "Ain't interested. Not at half the price."

"Four-fifty then?"

Whitby shook his head again, reassured by the grin on Grivitch's face and the feel of the derringer in the front of his overalls. "Mister, you know about horses you'd know that he ain't nothin' but dog food."

Grivitch turned in his saddle. "Bring them up here," he called to the other two. They pushed their shabby mounts forward. "How 'bout eight bucks the pair?"

Whitby shook his head. "They ain't no good. Wouldn't be worth their keep for the time they got left to live." He looked again at Grivitch's own mount. It was the best of the three, probably had a couple of years work left in him. "You really want to sell, I'll take that one off ya. Six bucks. With the saddle an' bridle."

Grivitch looked at him without moving then swung down out of the saddle. "You got a deal," he grunted.

As they made their way up the street, Grivitch on foot smoothing out the grubby bills, the man they called Cloud spoke. "Now you got no horse." His fat, yellow, tattooed face was screwed up in confusion. "What we gonna do? If we have to get outa here? In a hurry?"

"Relax, Cloud," replied Grivitch. "That never stopped us before."

They went first to Li Chong's eating-house and ate mightily. Towards the end of their meal they began cursing and complaining about the food. "What kinda shit you call this?" Wallace growled at the elderly Chinaman who waited nervously on them. "You expect us to pay for this crap?"

"You tryin' to insult us?" Grivitch shoved away a tin bowl of stew after eating more than three-quarters of it. "Feedin' us bad meat?"

"Food OK. No bad meat. All good. Food all good, very best." The old Chinaman shook his head, worried and afraid.

"You see him?" Grivitch pointed with his knife at the fat, yellow-faced man. "That's Joe Red-Cloud Mackin. Blood brother to the Shoshone. You give him bad meat he'll cut your goddamn balls off." He didn't say that Mackin's claim to brotherhood with the Shoshone was based on the fact that he'd shacked up for a month with a half-mad Osage squaw in an abandoned sod house outside Atchison, away back in Missouri fifteen years earlier.

"OK! OK! I bring other food. You wait." Li Chong saw trouble coming. He ran into his kitchen.

"Right! Let's go!" Grivitch shoved his chair back and lumbered towards the door, followed by Wallis. 'Red Cloud' stayed to slurp coffee, bending down to the table like a coyote drinking from a stream.

"No! You stay! You pay money!" Li Chong rushed out of the kitchen, a meat cleaver in his hand. He ran at Mackin and brandished the cleaver. "Money! You pay money!"

Mackin, grinning, threw hot coffee

into the Chinaman's face and, when he doubled up in shock, picked up a bottle from the table and hit him on the head. The old Chinaman went down. Mackin stayed long enough to stuff some bread into his pockets, then ran after the others. They were already riding up the street, pushing the two nags into an arthritic gallop. Mackin lumbered heavily after them, grinning hugely through mouthfuls of half-chewed food.

They twisted left and then right, right again and again left amongst Buckshot's crazy streets. After a few minutes they slowed down and finally stopped outside the Comfort House Saloon. They tied the nags to a rail and went in.

It was middling quiet. Two or three men stood at the bar drinking; card games were being played, without much interest, at three tables; two painted women moved around the room, not trying too hard for business. The entry of the three men went almost unnoticed.

They bellied up to the bar. "Whiskey!" called Grivitch.

"Yeah, me too." Ratbite Wallis thumped the bar.

Grivitch pushed him back. He nodded to the barkeep. "Leave the bottle." He took the bottle and three glasses and made his way to an empty table, Cloud and Ratbite with him. Grivitch poured and they drank and drank again and again one more time, then Grivitch stuck the cork in the bottle and they sat back and looked at each other.

"You in the mood for a little card sharpin'?" Grivitch looked at Cloud Mackin.

Mackin flexed his fingers. "I don' know." He wiped his hands on his thighs. "They wouldn't let me play with my cards. An' I ain't had enough practice lately to play with theirs. I could lose us all we got."

Grivitch snorted in disgust. "An' Jesus, that ain't much." He looked at Ratbite Wallis. "Looks as if it's goin' to be you, Rat. You up to it?"

Wallis shrugged. "Depends what the opposition's like."

"Let's find out." Grivitch rose and went to the bar.

"Any fightin' men here?" he called loudly. He looked around the room. Several men were looking at him. "You got any prize-fightin' men in this town?" He put up his fists in the manner of a bare-knuckle prize fighter. "'Cause I got one that'll whup 'im."

There was a faint rustle of interest. "Who's your man?" asked a customer at one of the tables. He wore town clothes and a greasy brown derby.

"Slammer Hodgson." Grivitch nodded towards Ratbite Wallis. "That's him over there."

All eyes turned to Wallis. He stood up and turned around, showing himself.

"He don' look much," grunted the man in the brown derby.

"He'll take anybody in this town." Grivitch spoke with complete confidence.

Several men had drawn closer. "Where

111

you goin' to fight?" asked one.

"Jus' outside, in the yard," shrugged Grivitch. "When?"

"Soon as we get a match."

The man looked around at the assembled onlookers. "We could get Pike Brady," suggested, his eyes shining with excitement. There was a murmur of approval. "Pike'll kill him," said another voice.

"What odds you offerin'?" the derby-hatted man called out from his table. More men were coming into the saloon.

"Even money," Grivitch called back. Two or three men went hurrying out as if bent on business.

"Even money? You ain't takin' no chances." The derby-hatted man threw a hand of cards down on the table and made his way to the bar. "Thought you figgered your man could take anybody in town?"

"I didn't know you had Pike Brady," grinned Grivitch. "We been hearin' about Brady in towns along the way."

"How much money you willin' to stake?" The derby-hatted man made a rubbing motion with thumb and fingers, as if holding money.

"Five bucks." It was all they could muster.

"Five bucks?" The derby-hatted man spat derisively. "Jesus! You ain't exactly . . . "

"For the first fight," Grivitch added hurriedly. "After that, well, we'll see. What I hear of Brady . . . "

"Well, take a look for yourself." The derby-hatted man turned round as a group of men came bustling in. "Here he is."

They were escorting him in like royalty, him in the centre, the others surrounding him. Small in stature, about five feet six, but stout and round and very, very solid, a close-cropped bullet head and an open, child-like face as yet unmarked by violent blows. The striking feature was his arms, long and angled at the elbow, like the arms of a gorilla. The expression on his face suggested excitement, childish pleasure and a good deal of confusion. "Where's the fightin' man?" he called.

Then they were all making their way to the yard outside. "You know him? This guy Brady?" Ratbite Wallis tugged nervously at Grivitch's arm. "You ain't lettin' me in for nothin', huh?"

"Relax." Grivitch was contemptuous. "Just a local pug. Use the bone if you have to."

Bets were placed and thirty men formed a ring in the bare, gritty yard. They waited to watch the spectacle. Pike Brady lumbered and puffed around, shrugging his massive shoulders, stamping the ground, his thick short legs like bridge stanchions. Ratbite Wallis watched him closely, licking his lips nervously.

A self-appointed referee in a shapeless pair of old army pants, a greasy vest and a coonskin cap called them together. "They ain't got to be no kickin' or gougin' or bitin'," he warned them. "Jus' fist fightin' — an maybe a li'l wrastlin', if it falls out that way. You git a li'l rest between rounds, but you fights to the finish. OK? Oh, an' the referee's decision is final," he added. "Now go to it."

8

They were circling each other, warily. Pike Brady's arms hung round his knees, monkey style; Wallis's were held high, like a prize fighter's. Two men, violently opposed to each other, locked within a ring that only one of them would emerge from in a conscious state, they circled each other like two fierce animals while the watchers breathed heavily, hungry for blood, pain and humiliation. Their boots scuffed menacingly on the gritty floor of the yard.

Nothing happened for a couple of minutes. "Aw, come on! Let's have some action!" called a voice.

"Yeah! You ain't here to dance!" called another.

Pike Brady responded, sweeping forward to the attack like a big, deadly spider. Quiet, smooth and very, very fast. Wallis swayed neatly out of the way, just as smooth, just as silent, and hit Brady a heavy clump on the ribs. There was a sound like a sledgehammer hitting sandstone and a gasp went up from the watching men.

Pike Brady was unaffected. He drew back swiftly and resumed his circling but suddenly surged forward again and struck. A long, sinewy gorilla arm flicked out like a snake's tongue, fast and deadly, and an iron-hard fist connected with Wallis's jaw.

But Wallis had been in many fights. He stepped back, letting his head roll and riding the punch. A half-step to his left and a sway away from the hips and he caught Brady again with another right to the ribs. Again there was the hammer-on-stone sound and another gasp from the onlookers.

"You jus' gonna let him hit you, Pike?" called a voice.

But the fight was just beginning. Neither of the men was marked or showed any distress. They circled more

117

briskly now, feinting and jabbing, both wary of each other, neither confident enough to press home an attack.

"Shit! If you're jus' gonna dance I'll go an' get Slim Jarrow from the saloon to play the goddamn piana!" called one man and there was a derisive laugh from the watching ring of men.

Brady swept forward in response, the spidery arms flicking out like tongues of flame and Wallis sidestepped, swayed and caught him with a thudding left hook to the face.

There was a sharp cracking sound and Brady stopped like a train that had run into the buffers. Wallis followed up with a right that caught him high up on the other side of his head, then Brady had his arms around Wallis and was crushing him in a bear hug.

They staggered around unsteadily, unable to control their footwork, now rocking this way, now that. Brady's nose and mouth were bleeding and a great fleshy bag of fluid had filled over his left eye but he had his head over Wallis's shoulder now and he was crushing the life out of him with those gorilla-like arms. Wallis's fists drummed on his back and ribs.

The breathing of the watching men was quicker now, harsher, almost lustful. The two gladiators struggled for advantage, heaving, pummelling, trying to keep their feet. Wallis's face was swelling, turning blue, Brady's a bloody, grinning mask.

Wallis, knowing that his situation was desperate, tried an old trick: suddenly he let every ounce of resistance go out of him, relaxing his whole body so completely that his legs didn't even hold him up; he let himself go completely limp, as if he had lost consciousness.

Brady stumbled, his concentration lost for a split second, and Wallis brought a knee up into his crotch. There was a hoarse gasp from Brady, a surge from Wallis and they were separate again.

Now the early preliminaries were over. Now fear, anger and the rage for revenge were rampant in the two men. Caution gave way to aggression.

Wallis was on the attack now, forcing Brady back, slugging at his head and body, landing heavy blows, trying to get in one really murderous punch. Brady retreated, fighting a rearguard action, the gorilla arms scything out with astonishing speed. Suddenly he connected. There was a crack like a pistol shot and Wallis's head snapped to the side as an iron-hard fist caught him on the jaw. He staggered for a second and suddenly Brady's great arms were encircling him again and he felt incredible pressure on his ribs.

Wallis knew he had to do something immediately. He caught Brady's chin in the cup of one hand and shoved ferociously backwards. Brady, threatened with a broken neck, released him and stepped back out of range.

"End of round one!" called the referee in the coonskin cap.

Wallis moved shakily back to his corner and sat on an upturned bucket,

Grivitch and Mackin hovering around him. "How you doin'?" asked Grivitch. "Think you can take him?"

"He's one tough bastard," panted Wallis. "I think maybe he already broke some of my goddamn ribs." He held out a hand towards Grivitch. "Gimme the bone," he said.

"Come out an' fight!" called the man in the coonskin cap and the two fighting animals were facing each other again.

It was a fight now, a fierce one, both men more intent on attack than on defence. Brady, sure of his strength, circled fast, sweeping in and out unpredictably, landing hard, punishing blows to Wallis's head and body. Wallis seemed to ignore them, moving fast himself, landing sledgehammer blows to Brady's body and his bloody, battered face. Few of the spectators noticed that these punches were all delivered with his left hand. In his right he nursed a smooth, hard bone, a three-inch cylinder cut from a buffalo spine where the ribs joined the backbone. The spine part nestled comfortably in his hand: three rib sections, growing out of the spine, reached out between his fingers, sticking out just proud of his hand to form a rough natural knuckleduster.

He couldn't use it yet, couldn't get in the punch. and the delay was costing him dear. Brady was landing too often, too regularly. Wallis had blood in his eyes now and he knew the fight was going against him. His breath was coming short; those hellish body blows were hurting him inside and he knew, the way a fighter does know, that the man he faced could, and would, destroy him.

Still he fought on, going from tight defence to daring attack. His own face was battered now and blood-covered, like Brady's; his chest heaved as he struggled for breath and his footwork was increasingly slow and heavy.

Brady sensed victory in his grasp. He swept in, hammered home a vicious right to the ribs then a left to the jaw.

Wallis almost stopped in his tracks, his guard dropping. Brady grinned through his bloody mask and swept in for the kill.

Then Wallis played his last card. A short side-step, a sway from the hips and a hammering right counterpunch. There was a crack like a dry branch breaking and Brady stopped in mid-motion. Wallis surged forward like a wolf going for the jugular. Another murderous right, two left jabs to the jaw of the tottering Brady then another pile driver with the right. Brady swayed like a tree that has been felled. Wallis measured his distance, stepped in to finish it. Brady, sinking to his knees, summoned the last dregs of his great strength, and swung one last punch, catching Wallis in the belly. Brady sank unconscious to the gritty earth and Wallis doubled up over him, groaning in anguish.

Several men moved over to them. "Let's have a look here," called the self-appointed referee excitedly.

"They's somethin' fishy goin' on here, you ask me!" He began to prise open Wallis's right fist.

"Shit! Leave him alone, Goddamnit!" Grivitch too lunged forward, shoving at the referee.

"He got somethin' in his hand!" called someone else. "He ain't been fightin' fair! He got knuckles of some kind."

The referee in the coonskin cap and Grivitch were struggling for possession of the bone. Cloud Mackin shoved forward to help Grivitch: two spectators rushed in to help the referee. A free-for-all fight was beginning.

"OK! OK! Git back, all of you!" A man with a shotgun had appeared and was forcing his way among them. The spectators fell back, recognizing his authority. It was Ward Gateley, deputy sheriff. "Now stand back, all of ya, so's I can see ya. An' you!" He shouted and motioned with the shotgun towards Grivitch and Mackin who were trying to drag Wallis off.

"You stay right where you are." The shotgun covered them unwaveringly.

"They been cheatin' on the fightin'," whined the man in the coonskin cap. "Been usin' knuckles of some kind."

"Yeah? I been hearin' about these fellas," drawled Gateley. "These the fellas, Li Chong?"

The old Chinaman was hurrying up to stand behind him. "Same men," he said. "No pay. Eat plenty. No pay. Throw coffee. Same men."

"Uh-huh?" Gateley nodded wisely. He looked Grivitch in the eye. "Saddle tramps, huh? You fellas think you can jus' come in here an' do jus' what the hell you like, don'cha?"

Grivitch shrugged. "Hell, we woulda paid him. Jus' had to git a li'l money first is all."

"An' you got the money now?"

There was a howl of rage. "They was cheatin'. Their man lost, by rights."

Gateley motioned with the shotgun. "I ain't happy about you fellas. Think I'll wait till I can make some enquiries.

Ed Borrows?" He nodded to one of the bystanders. "Take these fellas' weapons away from 'em and loop them over my arm. Easy now!" He cautioned Ike Grivitch with a motion of the shotgun as Grivitch appeared about to resist. "Don't go gittin' any ideas, 'cause I'll shoot if I have to. You don't want your legs cut down with buckshot, I'm pretty sure."

The man called Burrows moved carefully amongst the three men and collected pistols and shellbelts from Grivitch and Wallis as well as the long knife from Mackin.

"Say, what you got in that hand?" He looked at Grivitch with narrowed eyes.

"It ain't nothin'." Grivitch tried to slip the bone knuckles into a pants pocket.

"Hand it over!" Gateley motioned with the shotgun and Grivitch grudgingly complied.

"Just' an' ol' piece of bone," he shrugged.

"I guess," grunted Gateley. "An' you jus' carry it around for luck, huh?" He motioned again with the shotgun. "Now git movin'," he instructed them.

Grivitch grinned. "I can't move far. Got no goddamn mount."

"You can walk as far as the jail," spat Gateley. "That's where you're gonna be stayin' for the next couple of weeks."

9

When Gateley reached the jail, shepherding his three prisoners in front of him, he found Jim Parry hanging around outside the sheriff's office.

"Shit!" he spat. "What the hell do you want now?"

"I've found my horse," began Parry, "one of 'em, I mean."

"Aw, not now for Chrissakes!" groaned Gateley. "Can'tcha see I got other business? Here! Hold these weapons." He shucked the belts with their holstered pistols from off his shoulder and let Parry catch them, then, still covering the trio of prisoners with the shotgun, he took a bunch of keys from a board on the wall and moved to open a cell door. "Inside!" he ordered the three men. "All of you."

"Sheriff," began Grivitch, "we wasn't

doin' nothin' wrong. Honest. Just a li'l prize fightin'. That ain't breakin' no law. An' it ain't true what they was sayin'. We didn't use no bone knuckles or nothin' like that. It was a straight, fair fight."

"I believe you," Gateley snorted derisively and tossed the bone knuckle-duster on to the desk. "I suppose this is just a meat bone you been a-gnawin' on when you were hungry, huh?" He clanged the cell door shut and looked at Grivitch through the bars. "You got a charge against you. Chinaman's brought it. An' I don't like the look of you. Gonna hold you a while, till I can make some enquiries." He locked the cell door, hung the keys back on the board, put his shotgun in the rifle rack on the opposite wall and sat down behind the sheriff's desk. He leaned forward and put his face in his hands like a tired man, rubbing his eyes wearily. After a minute he sat back in his chair and looked at Parry. "What do you want now?" he asked.

Parry laid the two pistols and the knife on the desk. "I found one of my horses," he began, "an' I reckon the other one is right there too."

"Well you ain't got no complaint then." Gateley was curt, slightly contemptuous. "All you got to do is bring 'em back home."

"Well . . . I can't." Parry was tongue-tied, slightly intimidated by Gateley and finding it hard to explain the situation. "I mean, I know where my horse is, probably both of 'em. But those men have got them. They're still stolen — I mean, I know where they are but they've still got them an' I can't get them back. I tried, but . . . "

"Sweet sufferin' Jesus!" swore Gateley. "What the hell you talkin' about, mister?"

"I'm talkin' 'bout my horses. That got stole." Parry was growing angry now. "I tol' you about them before. Remember? I was in here. I tol' you, an' Sheriff Houghton."

"OK, OK!" Gateley gave a sigh

of resignation and drew a sheet of coarse writing paper and a stump of pencil towards him. "Now give me a description of the stolen animals."

"Well," Parry slowed down, the wind slightly taken out of his sails. "One's a buckskin, 'bout six years old, fourteen-three hands, shadin' to brown below the knee, mane kinda long. Other one's a bay, 'bout the same age, shadin' to dark on three feet, both fore and off hind. I don't know how long his mane is. It used to be long, like the buckskin's, but the buckskin's ain't long now so maybe they cut the bay's too." Parry stopped, feeling that he hadn't put his case very well, then he added, "They're both geldin's."

Deputy Gateley looked at him, shook his head and sighed. "Let's start again," he said. "Describe the horses. The buckskin first."

"I already told you."

"Tell me again."

"Well, like I said, he's a geldin'. About six year old. Nearly fifteen hands, used to have a long mane, used to shade to brown below the knee . . . "

Deputy Gateley threw down his pencil in exasperation. "What the hell do you mean?" he cried, "'*used to* shade to brown below the knee'? Is the goddamn animal dead or somethin'? I swear to Jesus, mister . . . ."

"Naw, he ain't goddamn dead!" swore Parry. "But I reckon they've dyed him below the knee. An' they cut his mane."

"Let's get this straight," sighed Gateley. "You say you've found a horse that was stolen from you, but he ain't exactly the colour of the horse you lost, an' his mane is different too. That it?"

Parry nodded. "That's about it."

"An' how the hell can he be your horse if he's different from the one you lost?"

"I reckon they've changed him, dyed him and cut his mane."

"You mean you've found a horse, a

buckskin, an' you've decided that he's yours, even though he looks entirely different."

"Naw!" cried Parry, "that ain't so. I know he's my horse! I know it! He's got a trick . . . "

"An' who stole this goddamn animal?" Gateley interrupted angrily. "If you know where he is you oughta know who stole him."

"I figger it was a man right here in this town. A Mister Samuels. He's keepin' the horses in a herd in a little hidden valley, eight – nine miles . . . "

"That does it, mister!" Gateley threw down his pencil stub. "I heard enough. Let me tell you somethin': that Mister Samuels you're talkin' about is a respected man in this town. He's been here for years, an' you've only just arrived. An he runs a respectable, legitimate business, right here in town. Anybody can go in there an' look around. I've been in myself. An' you come in here talkin' 'bout a horse that you *think* might be yours, an' you *think* might have been dyed — *dyed*, for Chrissakes! — an' it's kept in a little secret valley somewhere . . . "

"I'm tellin' you I know it's my horse!" shouted Parry.

"An' I'm tellin' you I got better things to do than listen to crazy ideas about dyed animals. I'm a-workin' on my own right now, Sheriff Houghton bein' away, an' I got serious work to do. Now get outa here an' don't come back till you got some real evidence. Go on, git!"

And Parry found himself outside, standing on the dusty porch.

He did not know what to do. He stood for a few seconds, breathing heavily and filled with confusion. Then he walked out into the street and along it, not knowing where he was going or why.

What in all hell was he to do? He didn't know. Couldn't think. In his mind he could hear Gateley's words: 'You've found a buckskin horse and you've decided he's yours, even though he looks entirely different'. Could that be true? One buckskin horse could look mighty like another. Maybe he was barking up the wrong tree?

In another part of his mind he could hear his wife's voice: 'Let it go, Jim! You're not the type of person for this kind of life. Let's quit this whole sorry scene, this awful place, these awful people and get out to California as quickly as we can. You're a store clerk, not a roughneck. Let it go. Please!'

He passed the Comfort House Saloon, Webster's Saddlery, Burrows's General Store, Harper's Forge. People were coming and going, women buying supplies, men conducting business, kids playing or trailing along after their mothers but Parry saw nothing of this, was unaware of the whole scene. He trailed his feet in the dust as he walked, muffled in uncertainty, confusion and misery.

What was the *right* thing to do? He'd do that if he knew what it was. But what was it? The law told him he was crazy, his wife told him he was unwise — and these were two sources of authority that he had always respected. Maybe he should listen to them? Take their advice? Maybe they were right?

Then another voice spoke in his head — his own. It said: 'I might be crazy, I might be confused, but I do know *some* things. I know I had two fine horses and I know somebody stole them. And I know that one of them's in that herd over by Eagle Ford. I know because it lies down when you tap it behind the quarters. And I'm pretty sure that that guy Samuels is the man behind it all. That's why he had me roughed up — to warn me off.'

He was breathing more quickly now, and becoming more aware of things. He stopped still, in the middle of the dusty road, to think things out even more clearly. His own voice continued to speak in his mind. "I know I had a good idea in that mule-train business. That would work well. I could make a good life for myself and my wife out here, in Buckshot. And those men who stole my animals, they've stolen all that from me. In a way they've stolen my life from me — and from my wife. She says to leave it be, just let them do it. But what kind of man would I be if I just let other men take my life — and hers — away from me without a fight?"

A woman passing at that moment was surprised to see him shake his head and say out loud — to nobody, as far as she could see — "Naw! I can't do that. I couldn't live with that."

He shrugged himself together and made his way to the livery stable where his mules were kept.

His saddle, the one he'd bought for the buckskin and the bay, was too big for the mule, didn't fit well. He tried putting on a double blanket but that didn't answer too well either. Well, that couldn't be helped. He tightened the cinches as much as he could and reached for the bridle.

As he was buckling the throat latch the Negro, Slowdrag, came in, shuffling his broom. "You goin' out, Mistuh Parry?" He watched him carefully, with wide, apprehensive eyes.

"Yeah." Parry was glad of the Negro's presence. It made him feel a little less alone. "Yeah, I'm goin' out, Slowdrag. I'm goin' to look at a horse I'm interested in."

"You buyin', Mistuh Parry?" The Negro looked slightly more cheerful.

Parry mounted the mule, settling uncomfortably in the awkward saddle. "Naw, I ain't exactly buyin'." He had a strange look about him, the Negro thought — sad, but hard and resolved. He took up the reins and spoke again, the words coming from between clenched teeth. "It's a horse I already paid for. I'm just goin' to collect him, that's all." And he rode out on the lean, leggy mule.

The trail to Nine Wells was easy riding, nothing to it, just sitting and letting the mule do the work, but when you left the trail the going got rougher and the further you went the rougher it got. His wife was right, Parry thought: this was wild country. Dusty sagebrush underfoot concealed a rough uneven surface that caused the mule to rock like a stagecoach over a bad road; deep hollows in the land, gouged by winter rains and snows, forced him to ride up and down steep inclines, making the mule sweat and pant and causing its rider to lean now forward now back like a monkey on a stick.

He wasn't even sure where the little canyon lay, just knew that it was out in that direction and near Eagle Ford. He'd found it once before and thought he could find it again.

It took him a long time and he felt he'd been lucky to find it the first time because it was easy to miss, a little concealed valley nestling in a remote fold of bleak, wild country. It was mid-afternoon when he found it and the mule was tiring and so was he. He dismounted and slackened the girths, tethered the mule to a bush, allowing it some slack to graze, and took some jerky from his saddle-bag.

He sat for a while, chewing and taking occasional swallows from his canteen. And thinking.

He could see horses in the distance. Just a few — two – three in a group — grazing easily. There'd be more, maybe twenty – thirty animals, he guessed, his own two amongst them.

What would he do? Well, he'd ride down there quietly, keeping a sharp lookout. He'd find those horses. And he'd just drive them quietly out of there, back home. It could be done. It just needed guts. He reckoned he had that.

But there were other things down in that valley besides horses: there was Brandy Lee, Jack Holt, and the man he had tangled with the other night — and probably other men like them. A hard ball of fear began to grow in Parry's belly. Those men weren't just men, they were animals — not manageable animals like mules or horses or dogs but dangerous, vicious animals — like wolves, or tigers — animals that would kill you without thinking, animals that would *devour* you.

He shook his head as if to empty it of such thoughts. He had been through all that already, in his mind. No point in going over it all again; it wouldn't come out any different. He took another bite of jerky that he didn't need and another drink of water that he didn't need either and then he reluctantly got to his feet. "Can't put it off no longer," he told himself grimly and, leading the mule, he began to walk slowly down the slope, into the secluded valley.

10

Leading the mule was a good idea, he told himself. He wouldn't be seen so easily, being lower down. And once he was amongst the horses he'd be pretty hard to spot.

He moved gently, looking carefully all around him as he went. Maybe he'd be lucky? Maybe nobody would see him? Maybe it would really just be a matter of moving in, collecting his horses and quietly driving them out. He found himself praying that it would be so.

He moved slowly and awkwardly, stooping low and taking advantage of every scrap of cover. Down a gradual slope he went, swishing through grass, his ankles giving on the uneven surface, the mule shoving into him from behind, almost knocking him over, flies buzzing blackly round his head.

He was close to the first horses now, two chestnuts and a grey, good animals, hard and fit. They ignored him. They were obviously well broke and used to people. He moved on and past them.

No more animals for some time, then a cluster of them, mixed bays, a couple of sorrels and that cute little palomino mare that he'd seen in the stables. There was no doubt about it, these were quality animals, all prime saddle stock. Parry's conviction grew. There was a horse-stealing operation going on here. Otherwise why would so many top-class animals be grazing in a little out-of-the-way valley? Horses like these were meant for use, for riding. They wouldn't all be resting at the same time.

He stopped among the bays. A couple raised their heads and studied him. Was his own among them? He was uncertain. He hadn't had his animals very long, and one bay looked pretty much like another. He studied each one closely and called the horse's name softly, "Rex. Rex. Rex." There was no response. A feeling of dismay washed over Parry: he didn't know his own horse; wouldn't be sure, even if he found it.

But hell! There was the buckskin! He knew the buckskin. He'd find that one at least. He moved on through the grass — good grass, little bluestem — his eyes on a group of animals some distance away. There were a couple of buckskins — or duns, maybe — among them.

He was in cover now, amongst some brush, which reassured him slightly. He moved more confidently. Now he was close to the animals. Two duns, nothing like his horse, a couple of chestnuts, two buckskins, a steeldust.

That was his! The buckskin with its head up, looking at him. No doubt about it. He'd found what he'd come for. "Scout, Scout," he called softly. The animal kept looking at him. He went forward, dragging the mule behind him.

He put his hand on the buckskin. It stayed put. He took it by the forelock and led it a little way from the group. It went easily. He tapped it behind the quarters. It hesitated. He tapped it again, insistently, and it began, awkwardly, to settle down on its haunches.

Parry thought for a moment then quickly unsaddled the mule. He transferred blanket and saddle to the buckskin, noting how well the saddle fitted. He took his rope from his saddle and formed a rough halter and lead rein for the mule, then took the bridle from the mule and put it on the buckskin. Every move he made told him that the buckskin was his.

He mounted, and now there was no doubt whatsoever: his legs *knew* the horse, recognized its gait. He began to ride forward, slowly, trailing the mule. His heart was beating fiercely. Now, if he could only find the bay and get the hell out of there!

He touched the buckskin with his heels and quickened into a canter. There were a lot of horses to look at. Maybe if he definitely saw his bay he'd recognize it? But he'd have to be quicker than he'd been so far. There was a large group grazing 2 – 300 yards away — bays, chestnuts, sorrels, greys, everything. He headed in that direction and saw a rider moving round them. Fear, sharp and sour, spread suddenly throughout Parry's being. And there was another rider slightly further off. While his mind was still taking this in, the first rider saw him, paused for a moment and then started to canter towards him.

Parry was suddenly riding the other way. Without thinking, spurred by fear, he had hauled his horse round and was riding full-pelt back the way he had come, the mule thumping clumsily after him and the shouts of the pursuing rider sounding in his ears.

Rough going. Thundering along at breakneck speed over the uneven ground, the buckskin grunting with the effort, its whole body like some great engine exercising its strength. Up a stiff slope, leaning forward over the horse's neck; down the other side, the animal slipping and sliding on its haunches, dust and stones flying up from the pounding hoofs, the shouts in his ears louder now, clearer.

The mule was hindering him, drumming along behind, all legs and ears and nearly hauling his arm out of its socket by its dragging on the lead rope. He could hear the drubbing hoofbeats of the pursuing riders. He let the mule go and felt the surge of increased power from the buckskin. Then a swift shade appearing on his right — another rider, from another direction — an impact like an express train, knocking all breath from him and the buckskin and the world tumbling upside down before his eyes, he was whirling through space and he was sliding on his back down a stony, dusty slope, dust blinding him, flints tearing his hands and face and then he was looking up at a blue-grey sky, clouds moving slowly across it, and he had a bad, bad feeling in his belly and he knew he had been caught.

★ ★ ★

He could see boots below batwing chaps near his face. Another pair of boots on the other side, below thick riding pants. Two men were standing over him. Someone else was picking himself up somewhere, cursing like a trooper. Horses were shaking themselves, panting, rattling their bridles.

"Well Jesus Christ! See who it is. It's the goddamn store clerk." A face pushed itself close to his and the fear stirred Parry's bowels as he recognized Jack Holt. Holt shoved a boot across Parry's neck, nearly cutting off his air supply, and drove his other boot on to his right arm, bestriding him and keeping him pinned to the dusty earth.

He called out, "Hey, Brandy! Guess who we got here! Friend of yours."

Parry couldn't move. Or he was afraid to. Or both. There was a scrabbling, a panting heaving and another man came up. A heavy, powerful, physical man. "Shit!" he spat and bent over Parry. "Holy shit!" He grinned happily. "It ain't him back again?"

"Yeah," Holt grinned. "Seems you run into each other again." He laughed at his joke. "Looks like you didn't teach him right last time."

He leaned down and grasping Parry by the hair hauled him to his feet. Parry felt as if his scalp must tear out.

"An' he's stole a horse," said Holt, not laughing this time.

Brandy Lee faked seriousness. "Yeah. I can see that. Well," he looked at the other two men. "We could hang him. We're entitled to do that. For horse thievin'. I mean, we warned him last time, didn't we? But he don't take no warnin's. We'd be right to hang him." He moved to a horse nearby and began to unfix a rope. Parry could see himself hanging from a tree, his body swaying in the wind, his face black, tongue sticking out. Brandy Lee held up a noose and draped it over Parry's head. He was grinning but there was hate and malice in his black eyes. He tightened the noose so that the rough rope scored Parry's neck and restricted his breathing. "Let's find us a tree," he said.

Holt waited a moment, savouring Parry's fear, then nodded. "Yeah. We'll hang him," he said. "But not here. We'll take him away a mile or two. We don't want him hangin' around." He grinned mirthlessly.

He grabbed the rope from Brandy Lee and dragged Parry over to where the horses stood. He mounted his own horse, a bony dun. Brandy Lee paused with one foot in the stirrup. "What'll we put him on?" He nodded towards Parry. "His mule?"

Holt looked down at Parry's white

face. "Naw. Let him goddamn walk," he said. He glanced at the third man. "Coober! Tie his hands." Coober looked uneasy but he silently took some rope and tied Parry's hands behind his back. They set off at a walk, Holt dragging Parry behind him.

He could keep up, just, if he strode out, but after a few minutes the strain and the uneven terrain made him stumble. Holt gigged his horse and dragged him ten yards over the rough earth then paused to let him regain his feet. "Looks like he ain't anxious to come along," he grinned towards Lee. "Come on!" he called to Parry. "Quit hangin' around. You got plenty of time to hang around later." And he gigged his mount forward.

It became a game, letting him walk a few paces then jerking him off his feet and they laughed and jeered as they played it. Parry panted and heaved for breath as the tightening noose restricted his air supply. The rough rope was already tearing the skin from his neck and throat. They meant to kill him, he knew that. He was going to his death.

The game grew more boisterous, the jerking off his feet more frequent. They began to drag him for longer distances. Finally, in a joy of excitement, Holt spurred his mount to a gallop, dragging Parry like an awkward log, rolling and bumping behind him while Lee pounded close behind, his mount sometimes actually treading on the living game.

Parry couldn't think. He was just a violent, blurred awareness — an awareness of fear, pain, confusion and the desperate need for air. He knew somewhere in himself that his face and arms and body were being torn and broken, that his eyes were filling with blood and his mouth was full of earth. He realized that he was praying, although he couldn't remember starting and didn't believe that it would do any good. His mind could only register thumps, collisions, fierce scrapings of his face and body and jerks that nearly tore his head off. He wouldn't hang — he remembered knowing that; he'd be dead long before it got to that stage.

Maybe they'd decided to kill him that way. They dragged him as if they meant to. At a furious killing gallop they rode. Holt's horse was frightened by the thing that bounced and rolled and scraped and dragged behind it and it jerked and shied erratically. Holt's reaction was to spur it more savagely, haul it round in frequent, savage changes of direction. Once Holt's mount stumbled and they reined in momentarily. "Is his goddamn head still on?" called Holt.

Lee rode up and looked down at the unmoving human cylinder on the ground. "Hard to tell, 'count of the blood," he called back. "It's half on, leastways."

"Other half to go!" whooped Holt and he dug his spurs into the sides of his heaving animal and the mad dance began again.

They didn't stop until their brutal energy had burned itself out. When they did they had covered two miles and what was on the end of the rope was a thing rather than a man. They were temporarily tired after their energetic game.

"There ain't no tree here," panted Lee.

"We'll find one," said Holt. "Jus' drag him a li'l further, is all."

"Hell, we don't need to bother." It was the man Coober who spoke. "He's goddamn dead already, you ask me. Or as good as."

They sat on their panting horses, looking down at the battered object on the ground.

"Put one in his skull?" Brandy Lee, reaching for his pistol, looked at Holt.

Holt was about to speak but Coober came in again, quickly. "I wouldn't. Anybody finds him with a bullet in him, there might be questions asked. Leave him here, cut the rope that ties his hands an' it looks like he fell off

154

his horse. Nobody asks no questions. An' he's still dead. Sammy might like it better that way."

Lee dismounted and drew his pistol. He put the muzzle close behind Parry's ear. "Maybe we oughta make sure," he said, looking up at Holt.

Holt sat silent for a moment then shook his head. "Naaa. If he ain't dead he soon will be. Ain't nobody goin' to come along an' find him here an' tend to him. Cut his hands free. Like Coober says, it'll look like he fell from his horse an' got dragged a bit."

Lee drew a knife and cut the rope that tied Parry's hands. They sat for a few minutes looking down at their handiwork then, when it didn't move, they rode off at a walk.

11

Deputy Sheriff Gately was walking back towards his office from Harper's Forge when he saw the two men riding up the street. Like all lawmen he took a good look at strangers and these were worth a look.

They were cowmen by the look of their rigs. Gateley stopped in his tracks to note them better for there was something about them, something that told him that these were men he'd have to watch.

They wore range clothes, like cowmen — leather batwing chaps, cowboy boots, flannel shirts, calfskin vests and out-of-shape stetsons — and they were riding prime animals, big cavalry-type mounts, one of them a stallion. They had rifles under their legs and shellbelts girdled their middles with big pistols showing out of holsters, but it wasn't their clothes, or their guns or horses which caused Gateley to pause and reflect.

It was their bearing. They rode quietly, without fuss, and they were not speaking but there was something about them, something almost tangible that said these men were entirely without fear. It was not the fearlessness of innocence, the kind that doesn't know fear because it had never met it: it was the fearlessness of men who have looked death in the face many times and who have developed contempt for it. It was the fearlessness of those who have fought life and death many times and have triumphed over them. These were men, Gateley knew in his belly, that, long ago, had gone way beyond fear. He felt an uneasy stirring in his bowels as he watched them.

They reined in outside the sheriff's office. They were calling on him.

Gateley clumped up the boardwalk. One of them, the one who'd been riding the stallion, was already waiting there for him. Not a big man. Around five feet seven Gateley noted with his lawman's eye for detail. Lean, spare and dusty. The other man was hitching the horses.

"Sheriff?" The lean man touched his hat in a courteous gesture. Again Gateley felt the strong deliberateness that emanated from him.

"Yeah. What can I do for you?" Gateley opened the door and nodded him inside. The Negro, Slowdrag, was just finishing sweeping the office floor, a task he performed two or three times each week.

"Name's Joel Shannon," said the stranger, following him inside. There was a clumping on the boards and his companion followed him in, another average-height, lean man, equally deliberate.

"This is my wrangler, Jim Silver," said the first man. "We're from Cook's County. Ranchers. I own the Curb Chain Ranch. It ain't the biggest, about eight hundred head, but it's healthy and we been there a long time."

Gateley nodded. "I don't know about ranches. Jus' the ones around here."

"Jus' to let you know who we are," said Shannon. His voice was quiet, courteous. "It ain't cows we've come about: it's horses."

"Yeah." Gateley didn't know why but he felt that he wasn't going to like what was coming.

"Stolen horses," said Jim Silver. Shannon looked at him and nodded. He turned to Gateley.

"Normally we wouldn't ride this far over stolen horses," he said. "It happens, now and again, a horse gets stolen. Guess it must be everyday stuff to you." Gateley was aware of two keen blue eyes looking at him penetratingly.

"Yeah," he said. "It's common enough."

Shannon nodded. He rested his buttocks against the desk, taking the weight from his feet. His hands just lay by his sides; he was perfectly relaxed, free of awkwardness, free of doubt. "This time it's somethin' different," he said, his voice quiet and matter-of-fact.

Gateley waited. He could hear the Negro, Slowdrag, pushing his broom around the cell area in the adjoining room.

"I'm lookin' for a particular horse, special animal," Shannon went on. "Little palomino mare." He looked at Gateley and when Gateley didn't speak he continued, "I bought the mare, 'bout a year ago. For my daughter." He looked again at Gateley and kept his gaze on him as he talked. "Fact is, Sheriff," he said, "my daughter ain't like other kids. She got somethin' wrong with her legs an' hands. They don't work jus' right. Co-ordination or somethin', they call it. She been like that since she was born. She's nine now."

"She'll be all right in time," Jim Silver put in. "When she gits more practice. When we git that mare back."

The ghost of a smile graced Joel Shannon's face. "Thank you, Jim. I guess you're right." He turned to Gateley again. "You see, Sheriff, the doc over in Goldwater figgered that if my daughter did some ridin' it might help her . . . eh, co-ordination." He pronounced the word with some difficulty. "Only she didn't get along with horses. Some folks don't. We couldn't get her started. Tried a dozen different animals but none of them was any good. Till Jim here found that little palomino. She took to that mare right off." A sad little smile played around his mouth. "Love at first sight, you might say. Took to each other straight away."

"An' it was doin' her good, real good." Jim Silver's voice too was soft and courteous but it too had that terrible deliberateness behind it. "Her co-ordination was gettin' good."

"Wasn't jus' that," Shannon interrupted his wrangler gently. "Wasn't jus' her movements. It was her whole outlook, her whole life. That girl was . . . well, kinda . . . born again, you might say. Took on a whole new attitude. Why she loved that mare the way she woulda loved a little sister. I never saw such a change in a . . . " he stopped, stuck for the word, "in a human bein'."

"This is the horse that got stole?" asked Gateley. He wanted to get it over with, whatever it was.

"Yeah," Shannon nodded. There was a silent pause then he spoke again, his voice full of a cold regret. "Somebody stole that mare." He eased himself off the desk and stood upright. "Sheriff," he said, "if it had been any other animal I wouldn'a cared much. The Curb Chain got plenty of ponies, some get sick an' die, some break a leg, some get stolen. Horse here or there ain't important to me. But this animal is. My little girl been sick ever since that mare was stolen. She's gone back months in her health an' there ain't a day passes but she's a-cryin' for that mare. An' there ain't nothin' the doc can do to help. She jus' gets sicker an' sicker. An' it breaks my heart, mister." He didn't look at Gateley this time. He looked at the floor, and a few seconds passed before he spoke again. "I got to get that mare back," he said simply. "Jus' got to. I've put the news around as well as I could but I ain't heard nothin' about it."

"What makes you think it might be around here?" Gateley asked.

"I ain't sayin' it is. I'm jus' lookin' everywhere I can, within sensible ridin' range."

"From Cook's County? That's seventy miles away. I wouldn't call that sensible ridin' range."

The blue eyes studied Gateley keenly. "No." The voice was still soft. "But then it ain't your mare. An' it ain't your little girl that's sick."

"What do you want me to do?" Gateley asked.

"You ain't found a horse like that?"

"No. We don't often get stolen animals brought to us."

"Naw." Shannon shook his head in mild disappointment. "I didn't think you would. Well." He hitched up his pants. "Maybe you'd keep your eyes open for that little palomino mare. Put the word around. I'd pay a good reward for gettin' her back. She's just under fourteen hands, clear palomino, golden yellow, cream mane and tail, about eight years old, I guess. She comes to the call of 'Gracie'. At least she does if my little girl calls."

"I'll ask around," said Gateley. "See if I can come up with anythin'."

"I'd be obliged," said Shannon. "Like I say, I'd pay a reward, a good one."

Jim Silver spoke. "Don't jus' ask the decent people," he said. "Ask the other kind, the kind who might know horse stealers. Tell them that we want the animal back an' that whoever's got it should bring it back to the Curb Chain, near Cook's County. We won't do nothin' to him."

"If I find a horse thief I'll put him

164

in jail," said Gateley defensively.

Silver nodded, gently. "Yeah. I guess that's what you would do," he said. "But if we find this one before you do, he won't be needin' no jail: he'll just need someone with a knife to cut him down."

And Gateley knew that he was stating a simple fact.

★ ★ ★

It was dark. He could see nothing. Or rather there was nothing to be seen, because he was lying face down on the earth. Maybe it wasn't even dark?

Maybe he was dead? How did you feel when you were dead? This could pass for it. His mouth was full of dirt. Had he been buried? Was he dead and buried? The sudden terrifying thought that he might have died and been buried alive electrified him and he knew suddenly that he was not dead.

But he was nearly dead. He was one

column of pain from his hair to the soles of his feet. Worst was his neck. He felt as if he was lying with his head and neck in a fire. Maybe he was? Maybe that explained it, maybe he had fallen and was lying with his head in a camp-fire? He tried squirming and thirty different kinds of agonies seared him like hot wires in thirty different places so that he had to stop and just lie there and burn — if that's what was happening.

But he could clear his mouth, maybe. He began to work his jaws, trying to push out the gritty earth. Then he was sick and the violent spasms tortured him so that he cried out. He heard the sound like it was from a long way off, the weak, pitiful squeals of a dying man.

But he wouldn't die. That sound goaded him. Someone had tried to kill him and weak rage surged in him at the thought. He was damned if he would die! He'd lie here and live, even if he couldn't do anything else! He'd just lie here and live, to spite them. He passed out again.

Next time he was aware that he could see grey light. Was he still in the same place? He felt exactly the same. But the light was welcome. He moved his right hand and found that it was close to his face. He felt for his neck and withdrew his hand in sudden fear as he encountered raw flesh.

There had been a rope around his neck. That came back to him with terrible clarity. And men had been dragging him behind a horse.

Maybe they were still there? Maybe they were above him, sitting on their horses, the rope still tying him to them? He tried to rise, crying with the pain, his muscles not working properly and him half expecting to be shot or knifed as he moved.

Grey light surrounded him, hills, bushes barely visible. Dawn, maybe? There was nobody around.

He was on all fours, still spitting out dirt. His clothes were almost completely torn off so that he was half naked, naked and kneeling like an animal. He could hear a sound, a low, dull ghostly howl and he realized that it was coming from himself: he was crying.

When he became conscious the third time he stayed conscious but he could only lie there. After an hour or so he realized that he was going to die if he didn't do something. The world was empty; there was nobody to help him and no help of any other kind. There was only him and Death there and only one of them could win. He realized that he was moving, although he hadn't given his muscles any orders; he was moving almost unconsciously, his body screaming with unremitting pain.

He had to stop and when he did he found he'd moved about six inches. But he'd moved. He rested then tried again.

So it went on, a few inches of agonized movement then a long rest, then a few more inches, then almost loss of consciousness, then another brief calvary. He had no sense of time but he knew that the light was going again before he came up against something hard and warm that moved powerfully and sent shock waves through his torn body. It made noises too, a ripping tearing sound and a fierce howling that sounded like demons in hell. He managed to clutch the warm object for support and found a warm, weedy wind blowing on his face. A great head with huge ears loomed before his half-closed eyes. One of those hellish demons? Then with a sudden, warm gratitude he knew what was happening: he'd found his mule.

* * *

Ross Samuels paced up and down the room, chewing on his cigar. He stopped at the window and stood looking out, rubbing a hand over his chin. Then he turned and looked at the other two men in his office. "You're sure he was dead?" he asked. "I mean stone cold dead?"

"He's dead," Brandy Lee growled contemptuously. "Coyotes have probably half-ate him by now. Couple of days from now he'll be coyote shit." He grinned at his companion.

"You too? You reckon he's dead?" Samuels looked at the second man.

"I couldn't say, boss," Jake Wilson shrugged. "I wasn't there. It was Brandy here, an' Holt. But if what they says is true . . . "

"He's goddamn dead!" Lee's voice was an impatient snarl. "Ain't nobody could've took that an' lived. He's dead, I tell ya. Stone cold dead."

Samuels nodded. "Well, dead men don't talk. I didn't want no more killin', not right now. But what I want even less is for that little bastard to come snoopin' around, askin' questions, talkin' to the goddamn sheriff."

"He ain't gonna be askin' no more questions."

Samuels seemed to decide. "Yeah. Right. Now listen. I want you to move that herd over to the place at Bald Hills."

"Now?" Lee seemed surprised.

"Naw. Not right away. I've got Grigor an' some boys bringin' in some more animals, in a few days' time. I don't want these animals in the stables here. There might be some questions asked about that little bastard who gave us the buckskin an' the bay. You." He turned to Jake Wilson. "You ride out west, over Woodville way, that's the way Grigor an' his boys will come. See if you can come up with them. Tell them to put the animals where the rest are right now. An' when they've had a couple of days' rest, move the whole herd over to our place at Bald Hills. I don't want no horses near me for the next couple of weeks."

"You want the whole herd, new animals an' all, moved over to Bald Hills? In a few days?" Jake Wilson frowned at his boss.

"Yeah. That's right. You got it." Samuels nodded sarcastically. "Now git goin'. Not you!" He grabbed Brandy Lee's arm as the stout man turned to go. "I got somethin' else for you to do. I want you to go back to where you left that fella and blow his goddamn head off."

"He's dead, I tell you, for Chrissakes."

Samuels spat out a shred of tobacco leaf and looked very deliberately into Lee's eye. "Then go back there an' blow his goddamn *dead* head off," he said. "But do it."

Lee met his gaze for a few seconds and seemed about to say something but then he dropped his gaze, turned around and clumped out of the room, swearing to himself.

★ ★ ★

A cowboy looking for strays found Parry. He was lying underneath a mule and he had a rope tied round his

172

wrist so that when the mule moved it dragged him along with it. The cowboy shook his head in horrified bewilderment. Then he lifted up the body, forced a little water between the torn and puffed lips and draped it across his own saddle. He mounted the mule and set off for a homestead he knew.

Parry's first clear impression, several days later, was of a log-and-sod ceiling. Further exploration brought the impression of log walls, a fire burning in a stone fireplace, people moving around here and there.

He slept for days at a stretch and dreamed that someone was feeding him soup from time to time and that once the soup was whiskey or brandy. He seemed to be there for years and gradually became aware that there were two kids, a boy and a girl and that their mother was there sometimes too and that a man came in at odd times although he couldn't think of what these people were to him.

Then one day his wife was amongst them. He was so surprised to see her that he spoke. "Hannah?" he croaked. "Is that you?"

She nodded. She'd been crying and her eyes were red but it was her all right. "Where am I?" he asked her, and she started crying again.

He was in a real bad way. There was no skin on his neck from shoulders to ears and his face and limbs looked as though he'd been pegged down in a field while they harrowed it. He had lost several teeth, some of his hair had been torn out, he was black with bruises from head to foot and there were great swellings in parts of his body. High up on the back of his right thigh there was the imprint of a horse's hoof, purple and livid, as clear as a brand.

There were psychological changes in him, too. He never moaned, even when they had to tear the sticking bandages away from his wounds or bend his swollen limbs, but he lay still and silent, not like a man dying but as though quietly co-operating with those who were trying to mend him. He spoke little of what had happened to him, beyond saying to his wife one day, "The men who stole our horses meant to kill me."

His wife reacted strangely. Before, she had entreated him to quit, to let things be, but now, though she wept a lot at first, she said nothing about quitting. It was as though she saw things in a different light: some men, it appeared, really were set on destroying her husband; that was clearly a fact and she could not blame him if he defended himself. They might have killed him this time; they might kill him next time; he could not be expected to permit them to do that. There seemed, to her, to be an awful inevitability about it. So when she found him out of bed one day, trying to get his pants, she did not remonstrate.

"You're sure you can do that?" she asked quietly.

"If I can't I'll try again tomorrow," was his reply.

It was a couple of days before he managed it, and a day later they left. Back in his own home he went straight to the lean-to shed at the back of his house where he kept the goods for delivery to his customers. When he came back he was carrying three new guns, a Colt Peacemaker pistol, a Henry rifle and a shotgun.

His wife watched with white, drawn face. "You aren't thinking of delivering those to the men who ordered them? You aren't thinking of going back to work already?" His neck was enclosed in thick bandages, one arm was in a sling and he could walk only with the help of a crutch.

"No." He had never owned a gun of his own. Had never used one. "No. I got somethin' to do before I can go back to work."

She didn't ask what it was: she didn't have to.

12

Cloud Mackin was standing looking out through the bars of the cell window at the dusty street outside. "Sure ain't much of a town," he whined. "Ain't nobody hardly ever passes. Dog now an' then. Rider, sometimes. Never no women though."

"What the hell you expect?" growled Ratbite Wallis from where he lay on his bunk. "You think they consider the view when they build a jail? Come away from them bars an' quit complainin', why don'cha. You been gripin' for a whole goddamn week. I'm a-sick of hearin' you yappin'."

"Aw, leave him," grunted Ike Grivitch sourly. "He ain't doin' nobody no harm." He wàs sitting on the edge of a bunk, his elbows on his knees. "What I'd give for the makin's," he muttered to himself. "Ain't had a smoke for a year, seems like. I wonder how long . . . ”

“Somebody comin',” said Mackin in a changed tone. “Comin' this way, looks like. Comin' right over here.”

His two cell companions showed no interest. “How long is that bastard sheriff gonna hold us here?” Wallis spat in sudden anger. “All this time, just over a fist . . . ”

“Comin' right this way!” Mackin interrupted him. “Man on a crutch! Arm in a sling too. Jesus! Looks like he been under a buffalo stampede.” He sniggered nasally. “Hey, mister!” he called suddenly. “You got the makin's of a smoke, huh? We sure could do with one.”

Grivitch and Wallis looked up with increased interest. When they heard a voice at the window they rose and moved to join Mackin. A man was standing there in the quiet street below, a man heavily bandaged, leaning on a crutch. He fumbled in a pocket and brought out a sack of Bull Durham and some papers. He waited till they had rolled cigarettes and dragged smoke desperately into their lungs.

"Jesus! I goddamn needed that," breathed Wallis.

The man nodded minimally. "I figured you might," he said.

Grivitch looked at the cigarette in his hands as he savoured the smoke. The tobacco was fresh, the papers new. He had the impression that all this wasn't just coincidence. He looked at the man, wondering how to frame the question but the man beat him to it.

"How'd you like to get out of there?" he asked.

Wallis and Mackin looked eagerly at Grivitch. Grivitch looked wary. He took another long drag at his smoke before answering. "What's the deal?" he asked.

"I'll bail you out. You help me to recover two stolen horses. Then you go free. That's the deal."

"Why us?" Grivitch asked carefully. "Why don'cha get the sheriff? Or other folks that ain't in jail? They'd help you."

"Sheriff don't believe me," said the man. His face was in a mess, as if he'd been in some kind of accident. "An' other people ain't the type of men I need. I need men like you. I gotta fight fire with fire."

"Say, who are you, mister?" Wallis spoke up. "You sound like you're lookin' for fightin' men, but you don't look like no fightin' man yourself. Or maybe you jus' ain't no good at it," he laughed.

"I'm a store clerk," said the bandaged man. "An' I ain't much good at fightin'. But then I only just took it up."

"Lemme think about this, huh?" Grivitch looked thoughtfully at the man in the street below and when the man nodded he withdrew back into the cell, taking Wallis and Mackin with him.

"What do you think, Ike?" Wallis was eager.

Grivitch nodded. "I think we gotta take his offer."

"But we don't know what we might be gittin' into." Mackin was less certain.

"I'll tell you what we do know," Grivitch cut in. "We know that any day now somebody could ride into this town from Grangeville or some of the other places we've been — places where we're wanted. We're wanted for horse stealin' — or jus' plain stealin' — in two – three places, an' you, Cloud, you're wanted for that knifin' back in Antler Bend. It ain't healthy for us to be held up here. We gotta get out."

"Well why don't we jus' let him bail us out an' hightail it outa town right off?" Wallis was pleased at his own suggestion.

"You forget I ain't got no horse," hissed Grivitch. "But if this fella's goin' after horses I might git me one of them. You fellas too, you ain't well mounted. We could all do with a good

181

mount. This could be our chance. Git ourselves good horses, maybe a little money, you never know. Then we can git goin' good."

"But these men he's figgerin' on goin' up against?" Ratbite Wallis was cagey. "You see the mess he's in. Looks like he been worked over. Maybe . . ."

"Shit! He's a goddamn store clerk!" Grivitch dismissed the protest. "Hell, his sister coulda done that to him. He's just a goddamn Mary Ann. What's tough to him ain't gonna be much to us." He looked challengingly at Wallis. "Unless you're scared?"

"You watch your mouth!" Wallis stepped up and put his face very close to Grivitch's.

"OK! OK! You ain't scared," Grivitch grinned appeasingly. "So how about it? You comin' with us?" Cause I'm takin' the man's offer."

"I'll go." Wallis tried to sound offhand. "Was goin' to, all along."

★ ★ ★

Slowdrag was shocked when he saw Parry. He watched him for several minutes before he spoke. "That you, Mistuh Parry?" His voice was musical with wonder. "What in the Lord you been doin', Mistuh Parry?"

"I guess you could say I been tryin' to get a horse, Slowdrag."

"Lord, Lord!" Slowdrag shook his head. "You oughta be in bed, Mistuh Parry." He cast a sideways glance at the three men with Parry and the whites of his eyes showed in unease. "You ain't wantin' yo' mule, Mistuh Parry?"

"I'm takin' four of 'em, Slowdrag."

The Negro hesitated. "You ain't figgerin' on ridin'?"

"I guess I am, Slowdrag. If I can get up I guess I can stay on. But I'd be obliged if you could lend me a saddle."

"Reckon Ah can, Mistuh Parry." The Negro trudged off into the harness room, shaking his head in great misgiving. He came back in a few minutes with an old Porter and heaved it on to the back of Parry's best mule. "Talkin' 'bout horses, Mistuh Parry," he mumbled as he worked, "maybe I oughta tell you, there was two men today lookin' for a horse — a li'l palomino mare. In the sheriff's office, they was. Mighty tough pair, you ask me. Want that mare real bad. They's offerin' a ree-ward for anybody finds it. Like I say, they's a mighty tough pair." The whites of his eyes showed again and he shook his head fearfully. "I wouldn't want to be the man who stole that li'l mare off them, no suh!" He tried a weak grin. "Seems like you ain't the only man with horse trouble, Mistuh Parry."

"Little palomino mare, huh?" Parry's voice was quick with interest.

"That's right, Mistuh Parry. 'Bout fourteen han's, maybe eight year ol'." He shook his head again in dread. "Ah cert'nly wouldn't want to be the man who stole that li'l mare, no suh!"

Parry nodded. "I'll keep my eyes open. Now could you give me a leg up into the saddle, Slowdrag?"

They rode a mile out of town, the others riding bareback, and then Parry stopped them. "You all got guns?"

Grivitch nodded. "All but Cloud here. You figure there'll be shootin'?"

"There might be some. Here," Parry turned and handed the pistol he was carrying to Mackin. The Henry rifle and the shotgun he kept to himself.

"What's the plan?" asked Grivitch. "How we gonna do it?"

Parry didn't waste words. "We're ridin' to a little canyon. That's where the horses are. There's about four or five men keepin' herd on them, but not all at once. Anyway, there's four of us, all armed. We're just gonna ride down there and pick out a couple of special horses an' drive them out there. If anybody comes along we'll just face it out. I figure we'll outgun them. That's why I brought you fellas along. There shouldn't be no trouble."

Grivitch nodded. "Since we're gonna be runnin' off a couple of horses, couldn't we make that five or six? Me an' the boys here are practically afoot."

Parry hesitated only a moment. "Mister, the horses in this valley are all stolen animals, two of them stolen from me. I ain't concerned 'bout the others, ain't gonna ask what happens to the rest, once I get mine. The others ain't no business of mine."

Grivitch grinned and looked at his companions. "Well, let's get goin'," he said.

"Hey! Hey!" Cloud Mackin grabbed Parry's arm as he was about to ride off. "Suppose these fellas — them that's herdin' the animals — suppose they shoots at us? Suppose they fight back? Real shootin' match?"

"Then you got to fight them, along with me." Parry looked him right in the eye. "That's what I paid your bail money for. Sixty bucks." He paused. "Of course you could always go back to jail."

"Naa. Shit!" Grivitch shoved Mackin

playfully to reassure him. "It'll be OK, I tell ya, Cloud." He turned his head away slightly and spoke to Mackin out of the side of his mouth. "There won't be no shootin'. Relax. He ain't the type to get mixed up in no gun battle."

Parry was already riding off and they followed him. "It's like I told you, Cloud," Grivitch murmured to Mackin as they trailed along in the rear. "It's small-time stuff. We do like he says, frighten these *hombres* a little and drive off some horses. Couple of days we'll be ridin' outa here, well mounted and full bellied. Maybe even a little money in our pockets." He grinned at Mackin reassuringly. "You can guess the kind of fellas they'll be. Don't take much to scare a store clerk."

The reassurance appeared to work, for Mackin became eager to get there. He and Wallis rode forward eagerly, getting further and further ahead of the other pair, who were slowed down by Parry's limited riding ability. "Take it easy!" Parry called several times.

"We want to get there in a bunch, all together." But Mackin paid no attention and he and Wallis were soon ahead by quarter of a mile. Parry peered after them anxiously. Hell! they didn't even know exactly where they were going. They could get goddamn lost if they got too far ahead.

Suddenly he realized that Mackin and Wallis had stopped. That wasn't like them. They didn't usually wait till the rest had caught up. Parry peered more closely into the distance. Was that smoke he saw hanging in the air, far ahead? Or dust maybe? Then he saw that Wallis had turned his mule and was riding back towards them. Something was wrong. "Come on," he urged Grivitch. "Somethin's happenin'."

They kicked the ungainly mules into a clumsy gallop. Ahead they could now see Wallis thumping awkwardly back towards them, calling out as he came, " . . . on the move!" he was shouting. "Think it's them . . . that herd. Horses, anyway. An' riders."

Parry rode past him without pausing and Grivitch and Wallis followed in his rear. Now he was closer Parry could see that what he'd seen in the air was dust, not smoke. A herd was on the move all right!

He reached the point where Mackin was sitting his mule waiting. "Horses!" said Mackin. "Think that's your herd?" He indicated a low valley 2 – 300 yards ahead. A small herd of about forty horses was moving towards them flanked by several riders. Dust rose in clouds around and above them.

"I don't know, for sure." Parry bit his lip in vexation. Was it them? He couldn't be certain. He hadn't expected them to be on the move. It might be another, a different herd. But this was the area all right. It was unlikely that there would be two horse herds in this area. He looked back. Grivitch and Wallis had joined them. "Let's take a look," he called to them. "But no shootin'. Unless they start it."

The herd was coming directly towards them, but lower down, about a hundred feet below them. They were approaching the neck of the valley where Parry and the others waited. A sharp incline led from the valley to the higher level, a rough, sandy slope punctuated by big rocks and stunted trees. It was bad footing; the animals would have to slow down, pick their way through the difficult terrain. "We'll wait here," Parry told them. "I'll tell you if it's them when they get closer. Spread out on each side of the trail."

13

There was the scuff and rattle of mule hoofs and the jerky, awkward movement of men and animals taking up position. The herd was getting close. Suddenly a shot rang out, and another. The approaching animals jumped in their stride and began to scatter. Parry, staring around, saw Mackin shooting wildly with the pistol. "You dumb bastard!" Grivitch was shouting. The herd had stopped going forward and was scattering outwards. The men herding it were riding up, fast, spreading out in a semi-circle. There were six or seven of them. "Into cover!" yelled Grivitch and he ran to the head of the sandy slope, among the rocks and stunted trees.

Parry was slow in getting down and he heard shooting, a lot of shooting. Something cracked the air as it passed him. It happened again. Bullets, he realized, and he let himself half-fall from his mule. He dragged himself down the sandy slope, expecting every second to feel the fierce, hot impact of lead smashing his bones and muscles. But he reached the cover and took shelter among a jumble of gritty, dusty rocks. Stone chipped viciously just in front of his eyes and he heard the whine of a ricochet. Jesus! He was in it now! he thought. A gun fight! A real gun fight!

He peered between the rocks at the animals a hundred yards away. He could see a big steeldust, half a dozen bays, two – three duns, a little palomino, couple of buckskins. It was the right herd, no doubt about that.

Lead cracked through the air above his head and a split second later a bullet ploughed into the earth only inches from his knee. He distinctly heard the soft 'duff' sound as it struck the ground and dust from it rose into the air. He saw in his mind what it might have done to his knee — saw lacerated flesh, smashed bone, blood everywhere — and suddenly knew that he could be killed any minute. Death was within touching distance. He could *feel* death hovering close by.

Huddled down amongst the dusty rocks, he thought for a few seconds. It had to come sometime, he thought. A man couldn't live his whole life in comfort and safety. Now his moment had come. How would he shape up? How would he acquit himself? Well, he'd do his best. Couldn't do no more, but he'd do that.

He drew a quick breath and wriggled like a snake, dragging himself further into cover, then brought his rifle up.

He'd never fired a gun before in his life. The incongruity of it all struck him as he worked the lever but he did not let that put him off: there were men out there who had tried to end his life and would do so again if they reached him. It was them or him.

He peered ahead between the gritty

rocks. He thought he could see part of a body showing behind boulders thirty yards in front of him. He pointed the Henry in that direction, squinted along the sights and squeezed the trigger. The explosion shocked him and the muzzle of the weapon jumped wildly. Nothing else happened. He fired again and kept the weapon steadier. Nothing happened. But men were firing, he could hear bullets cracking through the air above him and suddenly he heard an agonized yelp. Someone, somewhere, had been hit. There was increased shooting and between the explosions he could hear someone howling like a dog. The battle seemed to be coming closer. Grivitch was on his right, crouching behind a big boulder and shooting with his pistol. Parry realized with a shock that Grivitch was scared. His face was deathly white, he was gibbering like a demented ape and although he was shooting he was shooting wild and his whole body was shaking like a man with a fever.

Parry was shocked and disoriented by this realization. If Grivitch, a seasoned hardcase, was afraid then what . . . ? But he didn't have time for further thought. Suddenly two men appeared in plain view, thirty yards away, running for cover. Without thinking Parry pointed the rifle, sighted and squeezed. He heard the violent report and felt the kick and saw one man go down. Immediately he felt and heard bullets thudding into the rock in front of him, three or four in quick succession. He ducked and kept his head and his heels as low as he could. Bullets cracked over and around him and he could hear more crying.

The air was getting thick with gunsmoke. He risked raising his head a fraction and saw Jake Wilson, clear as day, twenty yards away and half-hidden behind a boulder. Wilson was fumbling frantically with shells from his belt and trying with shaking hands to reload a pistol. He didn't know Parry was there.

Parry raised the Henry, sighted and fired. Wilson looked up, saw where the fire was coming from and jumped up and started to run away. Parry worked the lever but, as he was about to bring the gun up, he saw Wilson fall. He got up again and stumbled forward a few yards then fell again.

The crackle of gunfire was continuous. A sudden yelp from close to Parry and he saw Grivitch drop his pistol and claw at his left arm. "Jesus Christ!" he squealed like a girl. "I'm hit! I'm hit! You bastard!" Parry saw Grivitch's eyes on him, wide with fear and hate. "You bastard!" he screamed. "You're gonna get me killed!"

There was the sound of rushing footsteps, boots scuffling quickly over loose sandy earth. Two men loomed in front of them, running like bulls and coming straight at them blasting with pistols as they pounded towards them. In the same instant Ike Grivitch, screaming like a horse in a burning stable, scrambled to his feet and ran, arms and legs flailing, blundering over rocks, falling and half-rising again to flee in mindless panic like a rabbit running from a coyote. Parry realized Grivitch was running away. Suddenly, caught in the fearsome panic, Parry too tried to turn and run but found that his bad leg wouldn't allow it and knew anyway that if he did he'd be shot in the back so he whirled back around and saw that one of the men almost upon him was Jack Holt and he fired the Henry point blank at him. Holt came thundering on but his eyes were rolling upwards, only the whites showing. Not knowing what he was doing Parry stood up and swung the Henry at a man right in front of him and caught him a solid, hammering blow on the side of the head. Bone cracked and the man slumped forward, crying. Parry dropped low again, chest heaving with fright, and shrank behind cover wishing that it was all over and had never started. The top half of a man's body was hanging over a boulder just in front of him and blood ran warmly and stickily down the gritty stone. The man was Coober.

The gunfire was slackening and Parry thought he could hear hoofbeats, as though someone was riding off, fast. But someone was still shooting murderously, keeping up a relentless fire. Then Parry heard a weird chattering, scrabbling noise from close by. He looked left and saw Ratbite Wallis and Cloud Mackin scurrying out from cover and running in the direction taken by Grivitch. Wallis was turning almost dementedly from time to time and blasting back with his pistol as he ran. Mackin was squealing in disintegrating panic and his arms and legs were working in odd ways as though he had lost all co-ordination.

They had all run away and left him. He was on his own now.

He accepted the fact and kept fighting because there was nothing else he could do. With fingers almost numb he reloaded the rifle. He looked around the side of his protective rock and saw a man half-sheltered behind a tree and shooting with a pistol. Deliberately ignoring the bullets that cracked past his head and thumped into the surrounding rocks, Parry aimed carefully and fired. The body jerked convulsively and the pistol fire ceased. Parry ducked behind his rock, worked the lever and looked out again into the firestorm for another target. A man was trying to work his way on his belly from one rock to another, perhaps trying to get round behind him. Parry shot him and ducked back down behind his rock. I'm still alive, he thought, but how long will that last? But the rate of fire was slower now, the din less terrifying. There was a sudden surge of blundering bodies, the hoarse rasp of panting breath and two men appeared on his left, surging round the edge of the rocks and shooting wildly with pistols. Parry fired the Henry from the hip, again and again and again and saw one man go down and the other turn and run. While Parry was firing at his retreating back a big heavy man loomed up among the rocks ten yards in front of him, a blazing pistol in each fist. It was Brandy Lee. Parry whirled round and fired the Henry at him but he knew that he'd shot yards wide. Then Lee was stomping straight towards him, guns spitting fire and lead.

Bullets cracked around Parry. He wondered if this was it and squeezed the trigger of the Henry. No explosion. No jerk of the muzzle. He squeezed again. Nothing. Lee was almost on him. He felt his bowels empty and dropped low, grabbing hysterically out for the shotgun. The heavy body of Brandy Lee surged towards him as he brought the gun half up and jerked the trigger. He heard the roar and felt the soft surge against his shoulder and saw the front of Lee's chest cave in. Momentum kept Lee coming till he fell over rock and collapsed at Parry's feet. The shooting had long stopped when Parry realized he was alone and still hitting the dead body with the butt of the shotgun.

14

Slowdrag was just coming out of the general store when he saw the little cavalcade approaching. A number of other people stopped to look too, because it wasn't something they saw every day. A man bedecked with dirty bandages was coming down the rutted-earth street in the middle of a knot of horses. He was riding a buckskin — or at least he was *on* a buckskin, because one leg hung stiff down nearly to the ground, as if he couldn't bend it and he seemed to be having trouble with one arm. The little herd of horses — there were four mules, a bay and a pretty little palomino mare — crowded round him as he moved forward, taking up the whole breadth of the street. There was something strange and rather frightening about the spectacle, though most people couldn't quite say what it was, except that they looked as if they were the survivors of some kind of battle.

"Lordy, Lordy!" Slowdrag let his breath out in a deep, soft sigh and made his shambling way to the livery stable.

He found the little cavalcade just arrived when he got there. "Mistuh Parry?" he enquired.

"Slowdrag?" the bandaged man nodded. "Would you help me get down?" The Negro obliged. It was an awkward process and took a few minutes to accomplish.

"Do Ah recognize them horses, Mistuh Parry? That buckskin an' the bay? Ain't them your animals? That you used'ta stable here before?"

"That's them, Slowdrag." The man seemed exhausted and to have trouble finding words and breath for them.

Slowdrag shoved his way among the mules till he came to the little palomino. "Pretty little mare, Mistuh Parry. Palomino, huh? Don't see many like her around. Ain't she jus' like the one they offerin' the ree-ward for? 'Bout fourteen han's . . . "

"She's the one, Slowdrag." The man seemed to gather himself, to make an effort. "An' you can do yourself a bit of good with this mare. Remember you told me about those men who were lookin' for this little mare?"

The Negro nodded. The whites of his eyes began to show.

"Well, you can claim the reward. All you got to do is find those men and tell them that the little mare they're lookin' for is in Ross Samuels' stable."

Slowdrag looked at the man carefully. "But you said . . . Ah mean." He looked from the palomino to the bandaged man. "That's the mare, you said . . . right here. How can she be in . . . ?" His brow wrinkled in a frown.

"Just you find those men, Slowdrag, and tell them that the mare they're lookin' for is in Samuels' stables. They'll find her there all right."

Ross Samuels was totting up accounts when his office door opened. He glanced up in irritation. He didn't permit people to just walk into his office. "Who the hell told you . . . " he began.

"Nobody." The man who entered said only the one word and the man behind him said nothing. They were cowmen, Samuels saw at a glance — the batwing chaps and the boots told him — and for some reason he didn't like them even though they had obviously come on business.

"Yeah? You oughta knock." Samuels decided that business must come first. "What can I do for you, gentlemen. You come for horses?"

"Horse." It was the second man who spoke. They were both lean, dusty men. Hard men too, Samuels decided. He wasn't sure what was going on.

"Just one horse," the first man spoke again. "Little palomino mare. *Stolen* palomino mare. Stolen from a little girl. My little girl."

Samuels felt he'd have to be careful. He shook his head in mock regret. "Yeah. Horses get stolen. I gotta watch, myself. Had two or three of my own . . . " His voice choked off as a lean hand reached out and grabbed him by the throat. He was hauled half-out of his chair.

"We found our little mare." The man held Samuels' face close to his own. He didn't raise his voice but held him still in the breath-choking grip. "She was hidden in your stable. Been there for a couple of weeks. You stole her, mister."

Samuels thought of the gun in the desk drawer. If he could just . . . He'd have to do something: these men would kill him. "No . . . no, you've got it wrong. I can explain," he choked. "You're makin' a mistake."

The grip was relaxed immediately. Samuels took a step backwards, gulped and began to straighten his shirt collar. "I

don't know about no palomino mare,"
he began. "Believe me, gentlemen. I
employ some men and maybe . . . "

"The mare's been in your stable.
Your stable, mister. Don't tell me that
a horse trader don't know what animals
he's got in his stable."

"I mean, well, I knew there was
a palomino in the stable," Samuels
improvised, "but I didn't know she
was stolen. I thought . . . "

"Wrong, mister," the second man
spoke. "There's been bills stuck up
all over town 'bout that mare. You
couldn't have missed them. And we
been askin' all round. Ever'body in
town must know 'bout that li'l mare."

Samuels glanced out of the corner of
his eye at the drawer that held the gun.
About four feet away. Could he . . . ?

"You're wastin' time . . . " The second
man spoke, a touch of impatience in
his voice. "That ain't like you, Joel.
You know this is the man. You know
'bout the other stolen animals, thirty or
forty of 'em. Let's do it." He stepped

forward and reached to take Samuels by the arm. A sudden shock of fear went through Samuels. There was no more time! He dived for the desk and got it half open before there was a deafening explosion and something in his chest seized his heart in a grip like a vice so that he couldn't breathe and didn't dare move. He half-lay where he was, something warm and wet running down his body inside his shirt. His shirt was staining red, sopping wet red, and there was gunsmoke in the air. Surely he hadn't been . . . The room seemed to be moving around him and growing fainter and fainter and he felt himself slipping to the floor and then there was just blackness and absolute silence and then there was nothing. Nothing at all.

Epilogue

It was a sharp, bright morning, nearly a year later, as Jim Parry rode out of Buckshot on his buckskin. Half a dozen mules tramped behind him fully loaded with merchandise and his bay horse brought up the rear of the string.

"Mornin', Jim." Ed Burrows, proprietor of the general store greeted him as he passed by. "You got quite a load there. Business good, huh?"

Parry reined in momentarily. "Yeah. Real good. An' gettin' better every day. How 'bout you, Ed?"

"Oh, can't complain," smiled Burrows. "You was right, though. Haulage business can't fail in these parts. Shoulda thought of it myself. How didja come to build it up? Come easy to you, did it?"

Parry grinned a little wryly. "Naw, it didn't come easy, Ed." He flexed his left arm, then his right leg as if there was some stiffness in them. "Like some other things, the basic idea was good but it needed a lot of workin' at, a lot of perseverance."

Burrows grinned. "Well, you'd be the one to do that, Jim. Ain't no one in this town got more perseverance than you, ever'body knows that."

Parry gigged his horse. "I gotta be gettin' along. Take it easy, Ed," he called. He looked back with a grin. "But take it!" he added.

Ed Burrows looked after him, shaking his head in gentle wonder. Jim Parry, for Chrissakes! One-time store clerk! Who'd have thought that he'd have built up such a business? And in such a short time? Well, maybe it wasn't so surprising. Parry was one to stick at a thing, once he started. Burrows grinned to himself. He was starting to be called Mulehead Parry in town, on account of his stubbornnesss, but people didn't like using that name to his face.

210

Parry was a nice fella, all right, but somehow he was also the kind of man you didn't want to offend. He wouldn't let nobody get away with nothin', that was for sure.

FIGHTING RAMROD
Charles N. Heckelmann

Most men would have cut their losses, but Frazer counted the bullets in his guns and said he'd soak the range in blood before he'd give up another inch of what was his.

LONE GUN
Eric Allen

Smoke Blackbird had been away too long. The Lequires had seized the Blackbird farm, forcing the Indians and settlers off, and no one seemed willing to fight! He had to fight alone.

THE THIRD RIDER
Barry Cord

Mel Rawlins wasn't going to let anything stand in his way. His father was murdered, his two brothers gone. Now Mel rode for vengeance.

ARIZONA DRIFTERS
W. C. Tuttle

When drifting Dutton and Lonnie Steelman decide to become partners they find that they have a common enemy in the formidable Thurston brothers.

TOMBSTONE
Matt Braun

Wells Fargo paid Luke Starbuck to outgun the silver-thieving stagecoach gang at Tombstone. Before long Luke can see the only thing bearing fruit in this eldorado will be the gallows tree.

HIGH BORDER RIDERS
Lee Floren

Buckshot McKee and Tortilla Joe cut the trail of a border tough who was running Mexican beef into Texas. They stopped the smuggler in his tracks.

BRETT RANDALL, GAMBLER
E. B. Mann

Larry Day had the choice of running away from the law or of assuming a dead man's place. No matter what he decided he was bound to end up dead.

THE GUNSHARP
William R. Cox

The Eggerleys weren't very smart. They trained their sights on Will Carney and Arizona's biggest blood bath began.

THE DEPUTY OF SAN RIANO
Lawrence A. Keating and
Al. P. Nelson

When a man fell dead from his horse, Ed Grant was spotted riding away from the scene. The deputy sheriff rode out after him and came up against everything from gunfire to dynamite.

FARGO: MASSACRE RIVER
John Benteen

The ambushers up ahead had now blocked the road. Fargo's convoy was a jumble, a perfect target for the insurgents' weapons!

SUNDANCE: DEATH IN THE LAVA
John Benteen

The Modoc's captured the wagon train and its cargo of gold. But now the halfbreed they called Sundance was going after it . . .

HARSH RECKONING
Phil Ketchum

Five years of keeping himself alive in a brutal prison had made Brand tough and careless about who he gunned down . . .

FARGO: PANAMA GOLD
John Benteen

With foreign money behind him, Buckner was going to destroy the Panama Canal before it could be completed. Fargo's job was to stop Buckner.

FARGO: THE SHARPSHOOTERS
John Benteen

The Canfield clan, thirty strong were raising hell in Texas. Fargo was tough enough to hold his own against the whole clan.

PISTOL LAW
Paul Evan Lehman

Lance Jones came back to Mustang for just one thing — revenge! Revenge on the people who had him thrown in jail.

HELL RIDERS
Steve Mensing

Wade Walker's kid brother, Duane, was locked up in the Silver City jail facing a rope at dawn. Wade was a ruthless outlaw, but he was smart, and he had vowed to have his brother out of jail before morning!

DESERT OF THE DAMNED
Nelson Nye

The law was after him for the murder of a marshal — a murder he didn't commit. Breen was after him for revenge — and Breen wouldn't stop at anything . . . blackmail, a frameup . . . or murder.

DAY OF THE COMANCHEROS
Steven C. Lawrence

Their very name struck terror into men's hearts — the Comancheros, a savage army of cutthroats who swept across Texas, leaving behind a bloodstained trail of robbery and murder.